Way

The living way. A progressive manual of short devotions intended primarily for the young, with additional prayers and a doctrinal introduction

Way

The living way. A progressive manual of short devotions intended primarily for the young, with additional prayers and a doctrinal introduction

ISBN/EAN: 9783741183188

Manufactured in Europe, USA, Canada, Australia, Japa

Cover: Foto ©Andreas Hilbeck / pixelio.de

Manufactured and distributed by brebook publishing software
(www.brebook.com)

Way

The living way. A progressive manual of short devotions intended primarily for the young, with additional prayers and a doctrinal introduction

THE LIVING WAY

A PROGRESSIVE MANUAL OF

Short Devotions

INTENDED PRIMARILY FOR THE YOUNG

With Additional Prayers and a Doctrinal Introduction

LONDON

J. T. HAYES, 17 HENRIETTA STREET, COVENT GARDEN

Preface.

THIS manual is designed to supply, in a concise form, suitable Devotions for the Young, and also provide what is sufficient for use in more mature life. The Prayers in the earlier portion, therefore, are intended as the foundation ; and these may be supplemented by the Additional Devotions, as occasion arises, when the habit of systematic prayer has been formed.

The endeavour has been made to provide a sufficient variety for persons in different circumstances, or of different habits and dispositions, so that each may select what he feels to be most suitable for him, and best expresses his personal desires and aspirations.

A brief exposition of the sacramental system of the Church has been prefixed, which is intended to give such instruction as is necessary for the intelligent use of the

Prayers, and to express the principles on which they have been drawn up.

The compiler desires to acknowledge the kindness of those who have given permission for the insertion of the Hymns which he has selected : the proprietors of Hymns Ancient and Modern, for No. 3; the Rev. J. H. Butterworth, for No. 5 (from Rev. R. R. Chope's Hymn and Tune Book); Cardinal Newman, for No. 6; the Rev. J. W. Hewett, for No. 7 ; the editors of the Hymnary, for Nos. 8 and 9; the Rev. Canon Bright, for Nos. 10 and 11 ; the Rev. V. S. Coles, for No. 12 ; W. Chatterton Dix, Esq., for No. 13; Messrs. Richardson and Son, for Nos. 14 and 15, by the late Father Faber ; and the late Dr. Pusey, for No. 16 (from the ' Paradise of the Christian Soul ').

He desires further to express his obligations to other authors and compilers whose works may have been in any way of assistance to him.

Contents.

viii CONTENTS.

OFFICES.

Instruction in Christian Doctrine and Practice.

There is One only God, a self-existent Spirit, without beginning and without end ; the First Cause and Maker of all things ; infinite in His Being and present everywhere though He is a Personal God ; almighty ; unchangeable ; perfect in Wisdom, Goodness, and Holiness.

In the One God there are, and ever have been, Three Persons, of One Substance, All equal, and All eternal together ; the Father Who proceeds from none, the Son begotten of the Father from all eternity, and the Holy Ghost proceeding eternally from the Father and the Son. This Truth is called the Doctrine of the TRINITY.

The Second Person of the Trinity, God the Son, having existed from all eternity with the Father and the Holy Ghost, came from Heaven more than eighteen hundred and fifty years ago, took on Him the nature of man of the Blessed Virgin Mary, and was born of her ; so that Jesus Christ is both God and Man in One Person. In Jesus Christ the Nature of God and the Nature of Man are united, and will never be divided. This Truth is called the Doctrine of the INCARNATION.

The Trinity and the Incarnation are the leading Doctrines of the Christian Religion, distinguishing it from all religions whatever ; all other Christian Doctrines depend upon these two.

Jesus Christ, God and Man in One Person, offered Himself as the One and Only Perfect Sacrifice for the sins of the world ; died on the Cross to finish that sacrifice ; and, after rising again on the third day, ascended into Heaven to present that Sacrifice for ever to His Father.[1] Thus mankind has been redeemed and reconciled to God, for the sake of the infinite merits of Christ's sacrifice.   This is the Doctrine of the ATONEMENT.

The RESURRECTION of Jesus Christ from the dead is the ground of the Faith of Christians.   He rose again by His own power ; and at the Last Day He will raise us also from the dead with our bodies, to be judged by Him for what we have done.   The good will then be taken to be with Him in Heaven, and the wicked will be banished to Hell with the Devil and his angels.

Jesus Christ, when He was on earth, founded a Society, which He called the CHURCH, the office of which is to bring all men to the knowledge of the Truth, and to provide them with all the Means of Grace necessary for their salvation.   This Church is called Catholic (that is, universal) because it is for all people, it teaches everywhere and in all ages the same Truth, it has the same Orders of Ministers, and it has always the same Form of Worship.   Jesus Christ is the Head of the Church, and the Holy Ghost is its Guide and Director.   Jesus Christ has promised that the Church shall never fail, and never as a whole cease to teach the Truth.

Christ entrusted the direction and government of the Church first of all to His Apostles ; and these first

---

[1] It is to be understood that at our Lord's Ascension His *human Nature* was lifted up to the glory of Heaven.   From all eternity He was in Heaven, as God : since His Ascension (not before) He has been there as Man also.

Apostles consecrated to the same rank with themselves other men who in turn continually consecrated
others ; and thus a succession has been kept up to the
present time. Those who belong to this Order are
now called Bishops, and they exercise the same office
which was exercised by the first Apostles. The two
other Orders of Ministers are Priests and Deacons,
and these can be ordained by Bishops only. No body
of Christians can belong to the Church unless they
are presided over by Bishops lawfully consecrated.

The Church is " the witness and keeper of Holy
Writ ; " that is, the Church, as Christ's Society, has
the charge of the Bible, and has decided what Books
are the True Word of God and to be considered
" inspired."

The Church has held several Councils to protest
against false Teaching, and to declare what is the real
Truth as taught by Christ and proved by the Bible.
The main body of Truth thus settled is summed up in
three Creeds ; the Apostles' Creed, the Nicene Creed,
and the Athanasian Creed. The Faith authorised by
the Church is called the CATHOLIC FAITH ; all contrary teaching is called "heresy." The Liturgies of
the Church, the substance of which has come down
from the earliest ages of Christianity, and the general consent of the great Doctors (*i.e.* Teachers) of
the Church, are further witnesses to the Catholic
Faith.

As Jesus Christ has taken upon Him the nature
of Man, He has appointed certain Means by which
men may be united to Him, and receive from His
life to their souls. The two most important Means
for this are the Two SACRAMENTS OF THE GOSPEL ;
(1) Baptism   (2) the Lord's Supper, or Holy Communion.

HOLY BAPTISM must be administered with Water " in the Name of the Father, and of the Son, and of the Holy Ghost." In Baptism we are made "members of Christ;" that is to say, we are spiritually united to Christ, so that His Life, Virtue, Power, and Grace flow from Him into our souls. In Baptism we are made "children of God;" that is, adopted into His family. In Baptism we are made "inheritors of the kingdom of heaven;" that is, have a right given us to the privileges of the Church here, and to a share in the happiness of the Church triumphant hereafter. But we may prove unworthy of our right, and so forfeit it. In Baptism we are made "children of grace;" that is, we are taken into the special favour of God for the sake of His dear Son. In Baptism we become "regenerate;" that is, we are "born again of water and of the Holy Spirit." In Baptism, Original Sin, that is, the sin in which we were born, is washed away by the Blood of Christ; and, in the case of grown-up persons, the Actual Sins which they have committed are also put away on condition of their Repentance and Faith. Baptism is also the Form by which we are admitted to be members of the Church.

Our Lord instituted the HOLY COMMUNION as the Sacrifice of the New Covenant, to be continually offered up as the Memorial of His One Sacrifice on the Cross, and that by it we may plead the merits of that His Sacrifice in union with Jesus Christ, Who by His Presence in Heaven is ever presenting His perfect Sacrifice to His Father. The outward part of this Sacrament is Bread and Wine; and these, when consecrated, are the Body and Blood of Christ which are the inward part. The Holy Communion is the chief Act of Christian Worship; no other Form of Worship, however valuable, approaches it in dignity and virtue, for it was ordained by Christ Himself.

Nothing can take its place, and in all ages of the Church it has been celebrated at least every Sunday and Holy Day. It is the duty and privilege of baptized Christians to attend the celebrations of the Holy Communion on Sundays and the greatest Festivals at least, and take their part with the Priest at the Altar in offering this Sacrifice. The churches in which we worship God are always constructed with a view to the celebration of the Holy Communion, and the Altar is their chief and most essential part. No one below the rank of Priest has power to consecrate the Holy Communion.

The Holy Communion was also ordained by Christ in order that Christians may partake of the Sacrifice, by receiving therein His Body and Blood under the Form of Bread and Wine. The Faithful (*i.e.* Communicants) so partaking, are most closely united to Jesus Christ, which He Himself expresses by saying "He that eateth my Flesh and drinketh my Blood, dwelleth in Me and I in him. As the living Father hath sent Me, and I live by the Father : so he that eateth Me, even he shall live by Me." In Holy Communion they are made one with Christ and Christ with them ; the Body and Blood of Christ are for "the strengthening and refreshing of their souls," and are to "preserve both body and soul unto everlasting life." But if persons presume to communicate when out of the grace of God through sin, they receive that Sacred Food to their own condemnation.

Jesus Christ "hath given power and commandment to His Ministers to declare and pronounce to His people, being penitent, the Absolution and Remission of their sins." This He did after His Resurrection, when He said to His Apostles, "Whosoever sins ye remit, they are remitted unto them, and whosoever sins ye retain, they are retained." This power is imparted in these very words to every Priest when he is ordained by the Bishop. Such Absolution is given in general terms, in answer to a general confession, at Morning and Evening Prayer, and in the Communion Service. Absolution is still further given in answer to a private and particular Confession made to God before one of the Priests of the Church. The Prayer-book of the Church of England recommends such private Confession as a special Means of Grace by which the penitent obtains the assurance of forgiveness, together with comfort and counsel ; his conscience is hereby informed and enlightened, and his spiritual life guided and strengthened.

CONFIRMATION was instituted by the Apostles, probably in accordance with the directions of Christ, as the completion of Baptism, and the sealing of the work wrought there by the power of the Holy Ghost. Formerly it used to be administered as soon as possible after Baptism ; but now that Christians are generally baptized in infancy, Confirmation is administered only to those who have come to " years of discretion," that is, who are able to distinguish Right from Wrong, and have a sufficient knowledge of the Christian Faith. In Confirmation, the Holy Ghost is given by the laying on of the hands of the Bishop with solemn invocation. The effect of Confirmation is to strengthen Christians against the power of sin, and to enable them to live holy lives. No one below the rank of a Bishop has power to confirm. By the rule of the Church of England no one is allowed to receive the Holy Communion "until he has been confirmed, or is ready and desirous to be confirmed." After Confirmation it becomes a duty to receive Holy Communion regularly ; at least three times a year, of which times Easter is to be one.

The COMMUNION OF SAINTS is that spiritual inter-course and union which all faithful Christians, both living and departed, have with one another, by virtue of their union with Christ, Who is the "Lord both of dead and living." This union, begun in Baptism, is continued and maintained chiefly by Holy Com-munion, and by mutual prayers and intercessions; by virtue of it we unite ourselves with the Angels and the Saints in Light, and they unite themselves with us in Worship and Adoration.

Without DIVINE GRACE we cannot make so much as one step towards heaven; and all that is good in us is the gift of God. It is the Sacrifice of Christ's death alone that has obtained mercy, grace, and salvation for us; we have no merits of our own apart from Him; and, since the Fall of Man, mercy, grace, and salvation can be obtained only through the Passion and Death of Christ.

God is willing to forgive all sins, even the greatest, on our REPENTANCE, for the sake of Jesus Christ, and in answer to prayer. The three necessary parts of Repentance are true sorrow, confession of our faults, and a firm resolution by the grace of God to amend. We must also be ready to make satisfaction to any whom we may have injured by our sins, and to for-give those who have injured us. Christ has appointed in His Church certain Means whereby forgiveness is specially conveyed and answered; these are chiefly Baptism, Absolution,[1] and Holy Communion.

No sin of man can be atoned for even by the most perfect life afterwards, if such a life were possible; it is the Sacrifice of Christ alone which avails to atone for sin.

---

[1] See above, page 6,

Short Prayers.

Before Reading the Holy Scriptures.

TEACH me, O blessed JESU, Divine Master, the True Word of GOD, that I may know the things which belong to my salvation, and may rightly apprehend the truth.

After Reading.

Grant, O JESU, that, like Thy Blessed Mother, I may keep all Thy words, and ponder them in my heart.

Grace before Meals.

✠ Bless us, O LORD, and these Thy gifts, of which, by Thy bounty, we are about to partake, through JESUS CHRIST our LORD. Amen.

Grace after Meals.

✠ We give Thee thanks, Almighty GOD, for all Thy benefits, Who livest and reignest for ever and ever. Amen.

When the clock strikes.

✠ In the hour of death, and in the Day of Judgment, good LORD, deliver us.

On going into Church.

O LORD, in the multitude of Thy mercies I enter into Thy house, and worship Thee in Thy holy temple, and praise Thy Name.

✠ Purge me with hyssop, and I shall be clean : wash me, and I shall be whiter than snow. Make me a clean heart, O GOD, and renew a right spirit within me.

Before an ordinary Service in Church.

✠ In the Name of the FATHER, and of the SON, and of the HOLY GHOST. Amen. Help me, O Almighty GOD, to worship Thee now in spirit and in truth, through JESUS CHRIST our LORD. Amen.

After Service.

Forgive, O Lord, all the idle thoughts I have had, and all the imperfections of my service ; receive my prayers and praises, through JESUS CHRIST our LORD. Amen.

To be used frequently.

O Blessed JESU, grant us the gift of Thy holy love, pardon of all our sins, and grace to persevere unto the end. Amen.

At waking.

✠ Glory be to the FATHER, Who hath created me. Glory be to the SON, Who hath redeemed me. Glory be to the HOLY GHOST, Who hath sanctified me.

On rising.

✠ In Thy Name, O LORD JESU CHRIST, do I rise from sleep : do Thou bless, guide and guard me, and bring me to everlasting life. Amen.

On going into bed.

✠ In Thy Name, O LORD JESU CHRIST, crucified for me, I lay me down to rest : do Thou bless, save and defend me, and bring me to everlasting life. Amen.

Morning Prayers.

I.

✠ In the Name of the FATHER, and of the SON, and of the HOLY GHOST. Amen.

Blessed be the Holy and Undivided TRINITY, now and for ever. Amen.

O MY GOD, I firmly believe that Thou art here present, and knowest all the most secret thoughts of my heart.

Come, HOLY GHOST, fill the hearts of Thy faithful, and kindle in them the fire of Thy love :

Send forth Thy SPIRIT, and they shall be made, and Thou shalt renew the face of the earth.

Our FATHER. I believe.

Act of Adoration.

I adore Thee, most Holy TRINITY, the Beginning and the End of all things; praise and glory be to Thee through eternal ages; blessed and magnified he Thy holy Name for all Thy unspeakable mercies to me, especially for my redemption and preservation, even to this hour. I desire to join with all Thy saints and angels in due worship of Thee.

Acts of Faith, Hope, and Charity.

O my GOD, I believe in Thee, and in all Thou hast taught us in Thy Word and by Thy Church, because Thou art True; I hope in Thy boundless mercy, because Thou art Good; I love Thee with my whole heart, because Thou hast loved me, and for Thy sake I love my neighbour as myself.

Act of Good Resolution.

O my GOD, I detest my sins whereby I have displeased Thy Majesty and rejected Thy Love, especially [*here name the offences of your past life*]. I repent of them with deep sorrow, and I resolve this day, and through my whole. life, to avoid them, and to shun the occasions of sin.

Prayer to Jesus Christ.

O JESU ! SON of the Living GOD, help me that I be not occupied nor delighted with vain or wicked thoughts.

O JESU ! SON of GOD, Who wast silent before Pontius Pilate, restrain my tongue, that I may speak only what is pleasing to Thee.

O JESU ! SON of GOD, Who wast bound for me, govern my hands and all my members, that all my actions may be overruled for my good, and Thy glory. Amen.

Act of Intercession.

O Almighty FATHER, bless, I pray Thee, all my relations and friends, especially [*here name those for whom you should pray*]. Prosper the work of Thy Holy Catholic Church, extend her borders, restore her unity, renew her sacraments, and endue her clergy with Thy grace. And may the souls of the faithful, through the mercy of GOD, rest in peace. Amen.

Here may be added the Collect for the day, or any other additional Prayers.

✠ GOD the FATHER, GOD the SON, and GOD the HOLY GHOST, bless, preserve, and keep me, now and evermore. Amen.

Morning Prayers.

II.

✠ In the Name of the FATHER, and of the SON, and of the HOLY GHOST.

Blessed be the Holy and Undivided TRINITY, now and for ever. Amen.

Our FATHER.   I believe.

ALMIGHTY GOD, Who dwelling in the highest heaven, yet condescendest to regard the lowest creature here upon earth, I humbly adore Thy sacred Majesty ; and with all the powers of my soul and body, do exalt and praise Thy holy Name, for the mercies and comforts of this life, and for the hopes and assurance of a better : for protecting me from the evils and dangers of the night past, and for bringing me safe to the light of a new day : continue this Thy mercy and goodness to me ; and as Thou hast awakened my body from sleep, so raise my soul from sin, that I may walk soberly and honestly as in the day, in all holy obedience before Thy Face.

Deliver me, O merciful GOD, from the evils of this day, and guide my feet in the paths of peace and holiness, and strengthen my resolutions to em·brace all opportunities of doing good, and carefully to avoid all occasions of evil, especially those sins [*here name the sins you are most afraid of*] which by nature and inclination I am most likely to fall into : and when through frailty I forget Thee, do Thou in mercy remember me, and revive me with a double portion of Thy grace and Holy Spirit, to maintain a more vigorous defence against Satan and his devices. Have mercy upon all men ; shower down Thy graces and blessings upon all the Church of Christ, on all my relatives (*my father, my mother, my brothers, and my sisters*), on all my friends, on the Clergy, and give Thy holy angels charge over them to protect them from sin and danger. Make me diligent in the duties of my calling, and grant that in all the changes and chances of this life, I may absolutely submit to Thy divine Providence. Let Thy blessing be on all my actions, and let Thy Wisdom direct my intentions, that the whole course of my life, and the principal designs of my heart, may be so ordered by Thy governance that I may do always that which is pleasing in Thy sight, through JESUS CHRIST our LORD. Amen.

Give me grace, O LORD, to do what Thou commandest; and command what Thou pleasest.

Give me grace to suffer what Thou permittest; and permit what Thou pleasest.

May Thy holy angel, my guardian, enlighten, guard and direct me, this day and through my whole life.

Glory be to the FATHER, and to the SON: and to the HOLY GHOST;

As it was in the beginning, is now, and ever shall be: world without end. Amen.

✠ GOD the FATHER, bless me: JESUS CHRIST, defend and keep me; the virtue of the HOLY GHOST enlighten and sanctify me, this day and for ever. Amen.

Evening Prayers.

I.

✠ In the Name of the FATHER, and of the SON, and of the HOLY GHOST. Amen.

Blessed be the Holy and Undivided TRINITY, for ever and ever. Amen.

O MY GOD, I firmly believe that Thou art here present, and knowest all the most secret thoughts of my heart.

Come, HOLY GHOST, fill the hearts of Thy faithful, and kindle in them the fire of Thy love :

Send forth Thy SPIRIT, and they shall be made, and Thou shalt renew the face of the earth.

Act of Thanksgiving.

O most merciful GOD, I thank Thee for all the blessings which this day, and through my whole life, Thou hast bestowed upon me, a sinner. Praise and glory be to Thee from me, and from all Thine elect in heaven and earth.

Ask for light to discover your Sins.

O HOLY GHOST, true Light, enlighten my darkness, that I may see and know wherein I have this day offended against Thee, in thought, word or deed. Give me grace, I beseech Thee, to be truly sorry for my sins, and so to judge myself now, that in the last day I may be judged with mercy, through JESUS CHRIST our LORD. Amen.

Then examine your conscience as to what you have done during the day, and whether you have offended GOD, in thought, word, deed, or neglect. The following questions may help you :—

Did I neglect my prayers last night, or this morning?

Have I been attentive at Service?

Did I go to sleep with any sin on my conscience?

Was I lazy in getting up this morning?

Have I left undone any of my duties to-day?

Have I been idle at my studies or my work?

Have I been disobedient to those set over me?

Have I been unkind, ill-tempered, or jealous?

Have I given way to impure thoughts, words, or deeds?

Have I eaten or drunk too much?

Have I been dishonest in any way?

Have I told lies, or been deceitful?

Have I been guilty of profane or bad language?

On Fridays and Fasts.

Have I indulged my appetite, or neglected to deny myself?

Have I been unmindful of CHRIST's sufferings for me?

On Sundays and Festivals.

Have I neglected to attend the Blessed Sacrament on this day when I have had the opportunity?

Then confess to GOD the sins you have committed, as follows:—

I confess to GOD the FATHER Almighty, to His Only-begotten SON JESUS CHRIST, and to GOD the HOLY GHOST, before the whole company of Heaven, that I have sinned exceedingly in thought, word, and deed, through my fault, through my own fault, through my own most grievous fault. [*Here name the sins which you have discovered, then add*]

Wherefore I pray GOD the FATHER Almighty, His Only-begotten SON JESUS CHRIST, and GOD the

HOLY GHOST, to have mercy upon me, to forgive me my sins, and bring me to everlasting life. Amen.

✠ May the Almighty and merciful LORD grant me pardon, absolution, and remission of all my sins. Amen.

> LORD, have mercy.
> CHRIST, have mercy.
> LORD, have mercy.

Our FATHER.   I believe.

Save us, LORD, while waking, and defend us while sleeping, that when we are awake we may watch with CHRIST, and when we sleep we may rest in peace. Amen.

Intercession.

I commend to Thy loving-kindness, O LORD, all my relations and friends, especially [*here name those for whom you should pray*], that they may be filled with Thy grace, and may always rest in peace under Thy defence. Have mercy on all sick and dying persons, on all who are suffering or in sorrow, and on all who are in error or ignorance, that they may know the things which belong to their salvation.

I pray Thee, also, for those who have departed this life in Thy faith and fear, especially [*here name those departed for whom you should pray*], that they may attain the fulness of rest and peace. All necessaries for them, for us, and Thy whole Church, I humbly beg, in the Name and through the mediation of JESUS CHRIST our LORD. Amen.

Here may be added the Collect for the day, or any other additional Prayers.

✠ GOD the FATHER, GOD the SON, and GOD the HOLY GHOST, bless, preserve and keep me, now and more. Amen.

Evening Prayers.

II.

✠ In the Name of the FATHER, and of the SON, and of the HOLY GHOST.

Blessed be the Holy and Undivided TRINITY, now and for ever. Amen.

Our FATHER.　　　　　I believe.

Ask for light to discover your Sins.

O MY GOD, sovereign Judge of men, enlighten my mind by the grace of the HOLY SPIRIT, that I may know the sins which I have this day committed in thought, word or deed, whether against Thee, my neighbour, or myself, and give me grace truly to repent of them.

Here pause and consider where and in what company you have been this day, and call to mind the sins you have committed.

AGAINST GOD. By omitting or neglecting religious duties; irreverence; wilful distractions, or carelessness in prayer; resisting divine grace; oaths; murmuring; want of resignation; pride. [*Pause and examine.*]

AGAINST OUR NEIGHBOUR. By rash judgments; hatred; jealousy; contempt; quarrelling; passion; cruelty; slandering; bad example; causing offence or scandal; want of respect or obedience. [*Pause and examine.*]

AGAINST OURSELVES. By vanity; human respect; lying; thoughts, desires, talking or actions contrary to purity; by intemperance or greediness; by sulkiness or impatience; by indolen   and not attending to the duties of our calling. [*Pause and examine.*]

Then confess to God the sins which you have committed, as follows :—

O GOD of infinite mercy, I confess with true sorrow all the sins of my past life, and of this day, especially [*here name the sins of which you have been guilty, then add*] I beseech Thee by the death and by the love of Thy dear SON to forgive me these sins, and whatever else I have committed against Thee, in thought, word, or deed. I resolve by Thy grace to forsake my sins, and earnestly strive to amend.

O LORD, our heavenly Father, Whose glory the heavens cannot contain, look down from the throne of Thy Majesty and behold me Thy unworthy servant prostrate before Thy mercy-seat, humbly confessing both the vanity and sinfulness of my whole life, especially the omissions of my duty, and commission of sin this day, wherewith I have so lately offended Thine infinite Majesty and Goodness, and so grievously wounded my own soul. For these and all other my transgressions, I most earnestly repent, and desire to bring forth fruits meet for repentance. And now, O most gracious GOD, I praise and magnify Thy holy Name, for Thy great and innumerable benefits, purely proceeding from Thy Bounty, wholly intended for my good, and particularly for preserving me this day in the midst of so many dangers incident to my condition, and from so many calamities due to my sins. Thou art my Creator, O my GOD and Protector. Thou art the ultimate End of my being, and supreme Perfection of my nature. Under the shadow of Thy wing is perpetual repose, and from the light of Thy Countenance flow eternal joy and felicity. To Thee be glory and honour, to Thee adoration and obedience, from all Thy creatures for ever. Amen.

Visit, O LORD, this habitation, and drive away from it all the snares of the enemy. Let Thy holy angels dwell in it to keep us in peace, and let Thy blessing be ever upon us, through JESUS CHRIST our LORD. Amen.

O GOD, Who art the Giver of pardon and the Lover of men, grant unto us, and to all Thy servants, both living and departed [especially . . .] a merciful judgment at the last day, that we, in the face of all creatures, may then be acknowledged as Thy true children, through JESUS CHRIST our LORD. Amen.

O GOD, merciful and faithful, the aid of all that trust in Thee, keep safely under the shadow of Thy wings, ourselves, our friends, and relations, and all believers, even Thy whole Church ; and bring us to those unspeakable joys which Thou hast prepared for them that love Thee and keep Thy commandments, through JESUS CHRIST our LORD. Amen.

Glory be to the FATHER, and to the SON : and to the HOLY GHOST ;

As it was in the beginning, is now, and ever shall be : world without end. Amen.

✠ GOD the FATHER, bless me : JESUS CHRIST, defend and keep me ; the virtue of the HOLY GHOST enlighten and sanctify me, this night and for ever. Amen.

Short Prayers for the Hours.[1]

Terce.

ALMIGHTY GOD, Who as about this hour didst instruct and replenish the hearts of Thy faithful servants by sending upon them the light of Thy HOLY SPIRIT; grant us by the same SPIRIT to have a right judgment in all things, that we may both perceive and know what things we ought to do, and also may have grace and power faithfully to perform the same; through the merits of our LORD JESUS CHRIST, Who was also at this hour contented to receive the bitter sentence of death for us, and now liveth and reigneth in the unity of the same blessed SPIRIT, One GOD, world without end. Amen.

For Peace and Unity.

VOUCHSAFE, we beseech Thee, O LORD, to grant to Thy whole faithful people, unity, peace, and true concord, both visible and invisible; through JESUS CHRIST our LORD. Amen.

Sext.

O LORD JESU CHRIST, the blessed SON of GOD, Who hast suffered death on the cross for us, that we might thereby be brought to eternal life; have mercy upon us, we beseech Thee, both now and at the hour of death; and grant unto us Thy humble servants, with all other faithful people that have this Thy blessed passion in devout remembrance, a godly and peaceful life in this present world; and, through

---

[1] These Prayers are suitable for use at the three Hours, as indicated; or otherwise.

Thy grace, eternal glory in the life to come, where, with the FATHER and the HOLY GHOST, Thou livest and reignest ever One GOD, world without end. Amen.

For the Conversion of Sinners.

ALMIGHTY GOD, we beseech Thee to hear our prayers for such as sin against Thee, or neglect to serve Thee [especially . . .], that thou wouldest vouchsafe to bestow upon them true repentance, and an earnest longing for Thy service; through JESUS CHRIST our LORD. Amen.

None.

HEAR us, O LORD, and remember now the hour in which Thou didst once commend Thy blessed Spirit into the hands of Thy heavenly FATHER: when with a torn Body and a broken Heart Thou didst show forth the bowels of Thy mercy, and die for us: we beseech Thee, O Thou Brightness and Image of GOD, so to assist us by this Thy most precious death, that, being dead unto the world, we may live only unto Thee; and at the last hour of our departing from this mortal life, we may commend our souls into Thy hands; and that Thou mayest receive us into immortal life, there to reign with Thee for ever and ever. Amen.

For the Advancement of the Faithful.

VOUCHSAFE, we beseech Thee, O LORD, to strengthen and confirm all Thy faithful [especially . . .] and to lift up their minds more and more continually to heavenly desires; through JESUS CHRIST our LORD. Amen.

Forms of Prayer

INTENDED FOR THOSE WHO WISH TO USE
THEIR OWN WORDS.

MORNING.

*On awaking, recall to mind the Presence of God;
thank Him for His past care; ask for His continued
protection.*

*On rising, resolve to spend the day to His glory,
and to promote the salvation of your soul, and the
good of others.*

✠ In the Name of the FATHER, &c.

1. Act of Adoration to GOD, almighty, eternal,
wise, good, just, and merciful; the FATHER Who
made you, the SON Who redeemed you, the HOLY
GHOST Who sanctifies you.

2. Acts of Faith, Hope, and Charity.

3. Recall GOD'S mercies to you during your
past life; thank Him for His benefits; pray Him to
continue them.

4. Think of your past sins, and those to which
you are most liable. Ask for pardon, grace to overcome them, and strength to resist temptation.

5. Think of special virtues to be practised, and
duties to be done; ask for assistance.

6. Offer intercessions for relations, friends, bene-
actors, superiors, inferiors, the Church, the Clergy
those in suffering, the dying, the faithful departed.

7. Occasional Prayers.

8. The LORD'S Prayer; the Apostles' Creed.

9. A concluding Form of Blessing.

EVENING.

✠ In the Name of the FATHER, &c.

1. Act of Adoration, as in the morning.

2. Recall the events of the day; ask for light to know your sins and shortcomings.

3. Examine your conscience as to your sins; in thought, word, or deed; against GOD, your neighbour or yourself.

4. Confess the sins and failings of which you have been guilty.

5. Acts of Contrition and good Resolution, in thought of GOD'S Love and Goodness, and your ingratitude to Him. Compare your life with what it ought to be, and with the life of JESUS CHRIST.

6. Pray for grace to amend your life, to increase in virtue, to practise holiness, to serve GOD and man, and to persevere unto the end.

7. Thank GOD for His mercies during the day. Ask for His continued protection during the night, and the guardianship of His angels. Pray that you may rise in health and strength, if it be His Will, and that when you die you may sleep in peace, and at the last Day rise to eternal life.

8. Act of Intercession as in the morning.

9. Occasional Prayers.

10. The LORD'S Prayer; the Apostles' Creed.

11. A concluding Form of Blessing.

Devotions for the Seasons.

COMMEMORATIONS OF THE |LIFE AND
PASSION OF JESUS CHRIST.

Advent.

I ADORE, I praise and glorify Thee; I give
thanks to Thee, O SON of the living GOD, most
gracious JESUS : Who didst at Thy first Advent take
our nature upon Thee to unite us to Thyself, and
restore us to the love and favour of the FATHER.
Do Thou, who camest to be our Saviour, prepare us
by Thy gifts of grace to meet Thee with joy at Thy
second Advent, when Thou shalt come again to be
our Judge.

O GRACIOUS SAVIOUR, of Thy Love and
Goodness, look upon me Thy humble servant;
sanctify me wholly ; give me full pardon of my sins,
and renew a right spirit within me ; grant that I may
imitate Thy humility, resignation, patience, charity,
and all Thy virtues, that I may be well pleasing to
Thee. And may Thy holy Name be blessed throughout all ages. Amen.

Christmas.

I ADORE, I praise and glorify Thee, and I give
thanks to Thee, O SON of the living GOD, most
gracious JESUS ; Who for me didst vouchsafe to be
born a feeble Infant in a stable, to endure the cold
of winter, and to be laid in a manger ; Thou didst
condescend to become poor and weak, that Thou
mightest make me rich. Behold, I fall down in

spirit before Thy holy manger, and adore Thee, my
LORD, the King of angels.   Hail, holy Child, GOD
most high, most gracious JESUS ; Hail, Prince of
Peace, Light of the nations, the long-desired
SAVIOUR !   O gracious SAVIOUR, &c.   (See above.)

Circumcision and Epiphany.

I ADORE, I praise and glorify Thee, and I give
thanks to Thee, O SON of the living GOD, most
gracious JESUS ; for that Thou wast circumcised on
the eighth day, and didst shed Thy precious Blood
for me ; that Thou wast manifested to the Gentiles,
when the Wise Men, having sought Thee by the leading of a star, came with great joy to Bethlehem, and
there worshipped Thee, offering gifts ; wast presented in the temple, and redeemed as a poor man ;
and there just Simeon and Anna the prophetess re-
joiced greatly at Thy Presence—and that afterwards
Thou didst flee into Egypt.   Thou didst humbly
submit Thyself to Thy parents Mary and Joseph,
and promptly obey them, although Thou wert the
King of kings, and the Omnipotent GOD.   O gracious
SAVIOUR, &c.   (See above.)

Lent.

BAPTISM, FASTING, AND TEMPTATION OF
OUR LORD.

I ADORE, I praise and glorify Thee, and I give
thanks to Thee, O SON of the living GOD, most
gracious JESUS ; Who, that Thou mightest teach
perfectly the virtue of holy humility, wentest to Thy
servant John, baptising sinners to repentance, and
though Thou hadst never contracted the least spot of
sin, wast willing to be baptised of him in the river

Jordan.   After Baptism Thou didst fast forty days
and nights in the wilderness, dwelling with wild
beasts ; and didst not disdain to be tempted of the
devil for my salvation.   O gracious SAVIOUR, &c.
(See above.)

THE MIRACLES, LABOURS, AND SORROWS OF
OUR LORD.

I ADORE, I praise and glorify Thee, and I give
thanks to Thee, O SON of the living GOD, most
gracious JESUS; That Thou didst preach the kingdom of heaven, heal the sick, raise the dead, and do
many wonderful works ; didst graciously converse
with men, and most mercifully convert them ; and for
thirty-three years didst endure for my sake, many
labours, sorrows, persecutions, with a most meek
and lowly heart ; that Thou mightest teach me most
fully by precept and example, to live justly and
holily.   O gracious SAVIOUR, &c.   (See above.)

For Holy Week.

INSTITUTION OF THE HOLY EUCHARIST.

I ADORE, I praise and glorify Thee, and I give
thanks to Thee, O SON of the living GOD, most
gracious JESUS ; Who didst humbly, upon Thy knees,
wash the feet of Thy disciples, and afterwards, in
inconceivable love, didst institute the Holy Sacrament of the Eucharist, giving Thyself to us in It.
O wondrous mystery ! that CHRIST should herein
give to us His Body and His Blood.   O gracious
SAVIOUR, I beseech Thee, by that unspeakable love
wherewith Thou hast so loved us, as to wash us
from our sins in Thy own most precious Blood—I
beseech Thee to grant to me a sinner to approach
this holy Mystery with fear and trembling, with

penitence and contrition, with purity of heart and spiritual gladness, that I may feel the sweetness of Thy most blessed Presence, obtain remission of my sins, and everlasting life. May all partakers receive It with humble reverence, in memory of Thy bitter Passion, to the everlasting glory of Thy holy Name, and to the salvation of their souls. O gracious SAVIOUR, &c. (See above.)

THE AGONY AND BLOODY SWEAT, AND APPREHENSION, &c.

I ADORE, I praise and glorify Thee, and I give thanks to Thee, O SON of the living GOD, most gracious JESUS; Who for me didst not refuse to be affected with deep sadness, and, through the bitter anguish of Thy holy Soul, to sweat drops of blood; to be irreverently seized by wicked men, ignominiously bound as a thief and malefactor, and to be led thus bound to the High Priest, unjustly condemned, shamefully spit upon, smitten, clothed in ridicule; to be mocked, derided, scorned, and blasphemed; to stand before the heathen Pilate, to be falsely accused, and to be dragged thence to Herod; to be mocked by him, and clothed in garments of ridicule. Oh, how hard and humiliating were those things which Thou, the King of Glory, didst bear so meekly, and without a murmur for me, a vile sinner! O gracious SAVIOUR, &c. (See above.)

SCOURGED AND CROWNED WITH THORNS.

I ADORE, I praise and glorify Thee, and I give thanks to Thee, O SON of the living GOD, most gracious JESUS, Who for me wast willing to be stripped and bound to a pillar, and most cruelly scourged, freely shedding Thy most precious Blood;

to be crowned with thorns, contemptuously mocked by sinners, blindfolded, smitten with a reed, shamefully spit upon and ridiculed. O gracious SAVIOUR, &c. (See above.)

CONDEMNATION AND CRUCIFIXION.

I ADORE, I praise and glorify Thee, and I give thanks to Thee, O SON of the living GOD, most gracious JESUS, Who for me didst not disdain to be condemned to death, and to be given up to the will of the Jews ; Thou didst not disdain to be grievously oppressed with the weight of the Cross, and to be intolerably afflicted on the way to Calvary ; to have Thy Hands and Feet pierced with the cruel nails, and fixed to the Cross, and upon it to endure for three hours the most bitter and inexpressible pains ; to be tormented with intense thirst ; to drink vinegar and gall ; and at length, after having poured forth all Thy precious Blood, to die. Thus with the most fervent Love hast Thou redeemed me, O most compassionate, loving SAVIOUR ! Thus hast Thou paid my debts, and expiated my sins. O gracious SAVIOUR, &c. (See above.)

THE MEEKNESS OF JESUS.

I ADORE, I praise and glorify Thee, and I give thanks to Thee, O SON of the living GOD, most gracious JESUS, Who for me didst suffer the most bitter Passion and the most ignominious death. Oh, what great love, what bright virtues didst Thou show us in this Thy Passion ! For when Thou wast despised, mocked, condemned, and crucified, Thou, the meek and innocent Lamb of GOD, didst not open Thy mouth to complain ; but, bearing all with a tranquil mind, Thou didst pray the FATHER for those who persecuted Thee and afflicted Thee with tortures. O gracious SAVIOUR, &c. (See above.)

The Easter Festivals.

I ADORE, I praise and glorify Thee, and I give thanks to Thee, O most gracious JESUS, SON of the living GOD, Who for me didst rise from the dead, and, after forty days, didst ascend in the presence of Thy disciples into heaven, and didst send down the HOLY GHOST upon them ; have mercy upon me, O LORD my GOD, and grant that, rising from the evils of the old conversation, I may walk before Thee in newness of life ; and being daily renewed by Thy HOLY SPIRIT, and confirmed and filled by His Presence, I may serve Thee with a pure and stead-fast heart until I come to Thy heavenly kingdom. O gracious SAVIOUR, &c. (See above.)

Saints' Days.

I ADORE, I praise and glorify Thee, and I give thanks to Thee, O SON of the living GOD, most gracious JESUS, for all the graces and virtues Thou hast wrought in Thy saints, who glorified Thy Name in this life, and are now with Thee in light and joy (especially . . . .) I thankfully commemorate the heroic piety of those who served Thee in hunger and thirst, in prisons and chains, on racks and in tortures; and I rejoice in the glory and happiness to which Thou hast advanced them. Give me grace to cele-brate their memories, and to emulate their holy conversation, till we all meet before Thy glorious throne, and with one heart adore the SAVIOUR of all. O gracious SAVIOUR, &c. (See above.)

For Friday.

I ADORE, I praise and glorify Thee, and I give thanks to Thee, O SON of the living GOD, most gracious JESUS, for all that Thou didst endure for

my sake, especially for Thine Agony and Bloody
Sweat, Thy ignominious apprehension and bonds,
Thy unjust condemnation, the buffetings, mockings,
and scourgings to which Thou didst submit for love
of me ; for the crown of thorns, the contempt, the
shame, the overwhelming sorrows, the Wounds, the
Cross and Passion, which Thou didst endure for me
a vile sinner ; for Thy Death and Burial, Thy glorious
Resurrection and Ascension. Oh, wash me in Thy
precious Blood ; grant me remission of all my sins,
and destroy in me all evil passions and affections.
Give me the spirit of mortification and self-renuncia-
tion, true humility, patience, meekness, charity,
simplicity, sincerity, and perfect control over my
tongue and all my senses, that I may be a man after
Thine own heart. O gracious SAVIOUR, &c. (See
above).

For Penitential Days.

O ALMIGHTY GOD, Who art plenteous in
mercy and compassion, and hast promised
forgiveness to all who turn to Thee ; have pity upon
me, and grant me the grace of true repentance for my
many and grievous sins. I have sinned all the days
of my life ; my tongue talketh vanity and falsehood :
my eyes are evil, prone to lust ; my hands are slow
to good, and my feet swift to evil. I have not done
Thy will, nor kept Thy commandments ; but I have
broken Thy laws, and despised Thy goodness. Spare
me, O LORD, for Thy mercy's sake ; deliver me from
the snares of the devil. Pardon all my sins, voluntary
and involuntary, and make me so to grieve for them,
that I may hate them ; restrain my unruly passions
with Thy holy fear ; preserve me from all impure
thoughts, all wicked words, and all unlawful deeds ;
cleanse me from all filthiness of flesh and spirit, and

keep me ever in the unity of Thy holy Church. Have mercy upon me, O LORD, for Thou knowest whereof I am made ; wean me from this world ; deliver me from all temptations, and so strengthen me with Thy HOLY SPIRIT, that I may never fall or be shaken again, but be made worthy of Thy adoption, and a partaker of eternal life ; through JESUS CHRIST our SAVIOUR. Amen.

Occasional Prayers.

Sunday.—O Thou Who as on this day didst rise again from the dead, and didst send down the HOLY GHOST the Comforter ; raise up our souls unto newness of life, and renew us daily by Thy Holy Spirit ; and save us, good LORD.

Monday.—O Thou Who for us men and our salvation didst come down from Heaven, and wast born of the Virgin Mary ; grant that we being regenerate, and made Thy children by adoption and grace, may daily be renewed by the HOLY SPIRIT, till we come unto the measure of the stature of the fulness of CHRIST ; and save us, good LORD.

Tuesday.—O Thou Who didst for three years minister to mankind, relieving their bodies and instructing their souls ; grant us all things that are expedient for our welfare, and needful for our salvation ; and save us, good LORD.

Wednesday.—O Thou Who wast betrayed by Thine own familiar friend ; grant us never to be false to Thee, nor to be overtaken in that sin which doth so easily beset us; and save us, good LORD.

Thursday.—O Thou Who as on this day didst institute the Blessed Sacrament, and also didst ascend into heaven; make us to partake of Thy Body and Blood to the salvation of our souls, and worthily to participate in that Sacrifice which Thou dost plead for us, where Thou ever livest to make intercession for us; and save us, good LORD.

Friday.—O Thou Who as on this day didst nail the sins of the world with Thine own Body to the Tree; blot out the handwriting of offences that is against us, and have mercy upon those who sin against Thee [especially . . . .]; and save us, good LORD.

Saturday.—O Thou Who didst as on this day lie in the grave for us; grant that our sins may be buried with Thee, and when we shall walk through the valley of the shadow of Death, let Thy rod and Thy staff comfort us; and save us, good LORD.

A Short Litany.

O GOD the FATHER, have mercy upon me, and keep my memory, that I may always remember Thy gracious benefits. Amen.

O GOD the SON, Redeemer of the world, have mercy upon me, and guide my understanding, that I may always know Thy holy Will, and what is necessary to my calling, and expedient for my salvation. Amen.

O GOD the HOLY GHOST, have mercy upon me, and so govern my will, that I may desire nothing but what tendeth to the love and glory of GOD. Amen.

Acts of Faith, Hope, Charity, and Contrition. [1]

Faith.—O my GOD, I firmly believe all that Thou hast revealed, which Thy Holy Catholic Church proposes to me to be believed, because Thou art Truth itself, which can neither deceive nor be deceived. In this Faith I desire to live and die.

Hope.—O my GOD, relying on Thy gracious promises, I hope by the merits of JESUS CHRIST, for the pardon of my sins, for grace to serve Thee faithfully in this life, by doing the good works which Thou hast commanded, and for eternal happiness in the world to come, through JESUS CHRIST our LORD.

Charity.—O GOD, I love Thee with my whole heart, because Thou art Thyself infinitely good, and infinitely to be loved, especially for Thy mercy in redeeming and saving us ; and for love of Thee, I love my neighbour as myself.

Contrition.—O my GOD, I repent with my whole heart of having offended Thee ; I detest my sins for the love of Thee [especially . . . .] ; I resolve by the help of Thy grace to avoid every occasion of sin.

For Increase in Baptismal Grace.

ALMIGHTY GOD, the Fountain of all goodness and the Well-spring of all divine graces, Who hast vouchsafed to regenerate us, being born in sin, by water and the HOLY GHOST in the blessed laver of Baptism, thereby receiving us into the number of Thy children, and making us heirs of everlasting life in the communion of all Thy glorious saints ; strengthen us, we beseech Thee, O LORD, with that blessed SPIRIT of Thine, the ghostly Comforter, and daily

---

[1] For longer Acts see page 99.

D

increase in us Thy manifold gifts of grace, the Spirit
of wisdom and understanding, the Spirit of counsel
and ghostly strength, the Spirit of knowledge and
true godliness, and fulfil us, O LORD, with the
Spirit of Thy holy fear, even through Him Who sent
down the SPIRIT upon His Church, JESUS CHRIST
our LORD. Amen.

Before Confirmation, daily.

O LORD JESU CHRIST, Who hast sent the
Holy Spirit into the world to comfort us and
to lead us into all truth ; I pray Thee that I, trusting in Thy love, and following Thy footsteps in
lowliness of heart, may so prepare and make ready
my soul to receive the graces of Confirmation, that I
may come with true faith and penitent heart unto
that holy Ordinance, and may obtain the fulness of
those gifts which Thou dost promise, for strength to
resist all evil here, and for the perfection of joy in
the world to come, where Thou livest and reignest
with the FATHER, in the unity of the same HOLY
SPIRIT, GOD for ever and ever. Amen.

After Confirmation, occasionally.

GRANT, O LORD, that we, who have been
planted in the likeness of Thy death through
Baptism, may also be partakers of Thy Resurrection,
and that preserving the gift of Thy HOLY SPIRIT,
Who hath sealed us in Confirmation, and increasing
Thy grace committed to our charge, we may receive
the prize of our high calling, and be numbered with
the first-born whose names are written in heaven, in
Thee our GOD and LORD JESUS CHRIST ; to Whom
be glory for ever and ever. Amen.

Before Communion : especially before a First Communion.

O LORD JESU CHRIST, Who dost vouchsafe to come to us, Thy unworthy servants, in the Blessed Sacrament of Thy Body and Blood, prepare my body and soul, I beseech Thee, to receive Thee in these most sacred Mysteries. Grant me such repentance for my sins, such faith in the Atonement made by Thee for them on the Cross, such full purpose of amendment of life, such perfect love to Thee and to all men, as shall enable me to receive Thee with the fullest benefit to my soul. LORD, I am not worthy that Thou shouldest come under my roof ; yet, trusting in Thy mercy, I presume to draw near to Thy altar. Vouchsafe, O LORD JESU CHRIST, in this Sacrament, to cleanse me, to heal me, to strengthen me, to refresh me ; and grant that when I have received Thee, I may never again be separated from Thee by my sins, but may so persevere in Thy holy way, that united with Thee here in Thy Sacrament, I may dwell with Thee hereafter in Thy glory, where with the FATHER and the HOLY GHOST Thou livest and reignest, ever One GOD, world without end. Amen.

On a Birthday.

ALMIGHTY FATHER, by Whose Providence I was as on this day born into the world, and of whose Goodness I have been sustained unto this hour, I thank Thee that Thou hast been pleased thus to give me being and life. Teach me to know to what end I was born, even to serve and glorify Thee, and do Thy Will here and hereafter. Forgive, O LORD, all the time which I have used amiss, and grant that as I have now lived . . . . years in this world, I may so pass those which remain to me, that after this life ended, I may dwell with Thee in eternal life in heaven, through JESUS CHRIST our LORD. Amen.

For the Anniversary of Baptism, see prayer on page 33.

In Sickness.[1]

O MERCIFUL LORD, the true Physician, Who with a word dost cure all diseases of the soul, and also those of the body when Thou knowest it to be expedient for the soul : heal me, O LORD, and I shall be healed in my body ; save me, and I shall be saved in soul also.   In Thee, O LORD, alone do I trust, for whatever good Thou art pleased to grant me.   Give Thou, therefore, strength to the remedies which are offered me, that they may be blessed to my restoration to health ; or at least, work in my soul patience to bear whatever Thou dost see fit to lay upon me ; through JESUS CHRIST our LORD. Amen.

Thanksgiving after Recovery.

THOU hast renewed my life and my strength, holiest, dearest Lord ; I thank Thee, I bless Thee, for Thy mercies are great, Thy love is without measure.   Thou hast dealt graciously with me who am not worthy of the least of Thy mercies.   O Thou Who hearest the prayers of those who cry to Thee, speak to my heart, I pray Thee, that it may even now die wholly to itself, and Thou only from henceforth live in it.   Come then, LORD JESU, come into my soul, reveal Thy presence, Thy love ; and let me never be separated from Thee my Lord and Saviour.   Amen.

---

[1] For additional Devotions, see page 93.

Before Study.

O INCOMPREHENSIBLE CREATOR, the true Fountain of Light, and only Author of all Knowledge ; vouchsafe, I beseech Thee, to enlighten my understanding, and to remove from me the darkness of sin and ignorance. Give me diligence in study, quickness of apprehension, capacity of retaining, and the powerful assistance of Thy holy grace ; that what I hear or learn, I may apply to Thy honour and the eternal salvation of my soul, through JESUS CHRIST our LORD. Amen.

Before Teaching.

O ALMIGHTY GOD, the Fountain of Wisdom, from Whom all Truth proceeds ; vouchsafe to shed the brightness of Thy Light on the darkness of my understanding. Thou, Who makest eloquent the tongues of those who want utterance, direct my tongue, and pour on my lips the grace of Thy blessing. Grant me readiness and clearness in teaching, and the power to inform the minds of others. Bless, O LORD, my instruction to the maintenance of the Truth, the edification of Thy Church, and the good of souls, through JESUS CHRIST our LORD. Amen.

For the Choice of a Vocation.

G UIDE me, O LORD, I beseech Thee, in deciding upon my future course of life, and give me grace to follow the indications of Thy Providence, that I may live, not only to the salvation of my own soul, but to the advancement of Thy glory according to the measure of Thy merciful appointment, and may receive Thy blessing in time and in eternity ; through JESUS CHRIST our LORD. Amen.

Before a Journey.

O GOD, Who madest the children of Israel to walk dryshod through the midst of the Red Sea, and who didst open to the Wise Men, through the leading of a star, the way that led to Thee; grant to us, we beseech Thee, a prosperous journey and peaceful times, that, Thy holy angels having charge of us, we may happily arrive at that place whither we are journeying, and finally at the haven of eternal salvation. Amen.

O GOD, Who broughtest Abraham Thy servant out of the land of the Chaldees, and didst preserve him unhurt through all his journeyings, we beseech Thee, vouchsafe to keep us Thy servants; be unto us our support in setting out, our comfort on the way, our shadow in the heat, our covering in the rain and cold, a chariot in our weariness, a fortress in adversity, a staff in slippery places, a harbour in shipwreck; that under Thy guidance we may favourably reach the place whither we are going, and at length return to our home in safety; Who livest and reignest One GOD world without end. Amen.

For Grace to follow Christ.

O LORD JESUS CHRIST, the only SON of GOD, Who wast given both to be a sacrifice for sin and also an ensample of godly life; Who didst bid us take up our cross daily and follow Thee; make, we pray Thee, the yoke of Thy commandments sweet, and the burden of Thy cross light, unto our souls. Conform Thy servants, O LORD, to the likeness of Thy Passion. Give us grace, O Eternal FATHER, that we may strive to keep the way of the holy Cross, and carry in our hearts the image of JESUS crucified. Make us cheerfully resign ourselves to Thy divine Will, that, being fashioned after His life-giving death, we may die according to the flesh, and live according to the Spirit of righteousness ; through JESUS CHRIST our LORD and only SAVIOUR. Amen.

For Perseverance to the End.

O GOD, Who hast willed that we, who are appointed unto death, should yet know neither the day nor the hour thereof : grant to us Thy servants that we may walk before Thee in holiness all the days of our life, and finally depart in peace, and die in the LORD ; through JESUS CHRIST our SAVIOUR. Amen.

For Purity.

O LORD JESU CHRIST, Who art pure and free from every spot of sin ; so fill me with Thy grace that I may be pure in heart before Thee here, and hereafter see Thee in eternal glory : Who livest and reignest with the FATHER and the HOLY GHOST, One GOD, world without end. Amen.

Prayer for a Friend.

PRESERVE, O merciful LORD, Thy servant [. . . .], for whose health, happiness and prosperity I humbly offer up these my prayers to Thy Sacred Majesty, beseeching Thee to grant *him* a persevering constancy in the Catholic Faith, and a safe passage through this life's dangerous pilgrimage ; that no temptation of the world, the flesh, or the devil may have the power to separate *him* from Thee *his* First and Only Good. Give *him* grace to correspond to that state and condition of life in which Thou hast placed *him* ; direct *him* in all *his* ways ; defend *him* against all *his* enemies ; and finally grant *him* a happy death and departure out of this world, and a speedy passage after death to the fruition of Thy eternal felicity. Amen.

For a Friend in Distress.

VOUCHSAFE, O merciful LORD, to afford the sweetness of Thy comfort to Thy afflicted servant [. . . .], and to remove, according to Thy accustomed mercy, the heavy burden of *his* calamities. Give *him*, I humbly beseech Thee, patience in *his* sufferings, resignation to Thy good pleasure, perseverance in Thy service, and a happy translation from this afflicting life to Thy eternal felicity. Amen.

For the Conversion of another to the Faith of the Church.

O DIVINE and adorable SAVIOUR, Thou Who art the Way, the Truth, and the Life, I beseech Thee to have mercy upon [. . . .], and bring *him* to the knowledge and love of Thy truth. Thou, O LORD, knowest all *his* darkness, *his* weakness, and *his* doubts; have pity upon *him*, O merciful SAVIOUR; let the bright beams of Thy eternal truth shine upon *his* mind; clear away the cloud of error and prejudice from before *his* eyes, and may *he* humbly submit to, and embrace with *his* whole heart, the teaching of Thy Church. Oh, let not the soul for whom I pray be shut out from Thy blessed fold ! Unite *him* to Thyself in the sacraments of Thy love, and grant that, partaking of the blessings of Thy grace in this life, *he* may come at last to the possession of those eternal rewards which Thou hast promised to all those who believe in Thee and who do Thy Will. Hear this my petition, O merciful JESUS, Who, with the FATHER and the HOLY GHOST, livest and reignest ever and ever. Amen.

For the Sick.

℣. Heal Thy servants, O LORD, who are sick, and who put their trust in Thee.

℞. Send them help, O LORD, and comfort them from Thy holy place.

O ALMIGHTY and everlasting GOD, the eternal Salvation of them that trust in Thee, hear us in behalf of Thy servants who are sick ; for whom we humbly crave the help of Thy mercy ; that, their health being restored to them, they may render thanks to Thee in Thy Church ; through JESUS CHRIST our LORD. Amen.

For the Sick and Dying.

O GRACIOUS LORD JESUS, Who didst vouchsafe to die on the Cross for us ; remember, we beseech Thee, all sick and dying persons [especially . . . .], and grant that they may omit nothing which is necessary to make their peace with Thee before they die. Deliver them, O LORD, from the malice and treachery of the devil, and from all sin and evil ; and grant them a happy end, for Thy loving mercy's sake. Amen.

For those with whom we have sinned.

A LMIGHTY and merciful GOD, in deep humility and fear, and in sorrow of heart, I crave Thy mercy for those with whom I have sinned, or whom I have, knowingly or unknowingly, wilfully or ignorantly, by example or by neglect, been the means of leading into sin [especially . . . .]. Let not the guilt of their ruin be added to my shame and confusion at my own manifold offences and transgressions against Thee. As they have shared in my sin, may they also share in my repentance. Require not, I pray Thee, their blood at my hands, but forgive us all our sins, and grant that we may escape Thy condemnation, and of Thy mercy attain Thine eternal rewards, through the merits and mediation of JESUS CHRIST our SAVIOUR. Amen.

A General Intercession.

ALMIGHTY and everlasting GOD, Who makest us both to will and to do those things which are good and acceptable to Thy Divine Majesty, we make our humble supplications unto Thee in behalf of all our relations, friends, and acquaintances [especially . . . .]. Let Thy fatherly hand, we beseech Thee, ever be over them; let Thy HOLY SPIRIT ever be with them; and so lead them in the knowledge and obedience of Thy Word, that in the end they may obtain everlasting life. Have mercy upon this place [or parish]. Bless Thy holy Church; convert all blind and miserable sinners; bring back all heretics and schismatics; enlighten the ignorant; restore the backsliding; comfort the sorrowful, and succour all who are tempted or afflicted in mind, body, or estate. Pity, O LORD, and have mercy upon all men, for JESUS CHRIST'S sake, Who, with Thee and the HOLY GHOST, liveth and reigneth ever One GOD, world without end. Amen.

Another.

O GOD, merciful and faithful, the aid of all that trust in Thee, keep safely under the shadow of Thy wings ourselves, our relations, and friends [especially . . . .], and all believers, even Thy whole Church, that we may enjoy Thy Presence alway, and increase in Thy HOLY SPIRIT more and more, till we come to Thine everlasting kingdom. Succour the dying, comfort and heal the sick, succour all who are in trouble, sorrow, need, temptation, or any other adversity; and have mercy upon all for whom Thou hast shed Thy precious Blood. Have mercy upon this place, and grant that humility and meekness, peace and charity, chastity and purity may rule therein. Grant that we may so correct and amend ourselves, that we may love, and fear, and serve Thee faithfully all our days; through our LORD and SAVIOUR JESUS CHRIST. Amen.

For the Faithful departed.

℣. Eternal rest give to them, O LORD:
℟. And let light perpetual shine upon them.

O GOD, by Whose mercy the souls of the faithful find rest, grant unto all Thy servants that have slept in CHRIST [especially . . . .] eternal repose and light perpetual, that being discharged from all guilt, they may rejoice with Thee for all eternity; through JESUS CHRIST our LORD. Amen.

For Parents departed.

O GOD, Who hast commanded us to honour our father and mother, of Thy loving-kindness have mercy upon the souls of my *father and mother*, and grant that I may live with them in everlasting joy; through JESUS CHRIST our LORD. Amen.

For a Parish.

A LMIGHTY and everlasting GOD, Who dost govern all things in heaven and earth, mercifully hear the supplications of us Thy servants, and grant unto this Parish all things that are needful for its spiritual welfare [especially . . . .]. Strengthen and confirm the faithful; visit and relieve the sick; turn and soften the wicked; rouse the careless; recover the fallen; restore the penitent; remove all hindrances to the advancement of Thy Truth, and bring all to be of one heart and mind within the fold of Thy Holy Church, to the honour and glory of Thy blessed SON, JESUS CHRIST our LORD.   Amen.

For Brotherhoods and Sisterhoods.

VOUCHSAFE, we beseech Thee, merciful LORD, to prosper with Thy blessing the work of [. . . .] and all others designed to promote Thy glory and the good of souls.   Grant that those who serve Thee there, may set Thy holy Will ever before them, and do that which is well-pleasing in Thy sight, and persevere in Thy service unto the end ; through JESUS CHRIST our LORD.   Amen.

For Bishops and Clergy.

O LORD JESU CHRIST, Thou great Shepherd and Bishop of our souls, send down upon Thy servants, the Bishops and Pastors of Thy Church [especially . . . .] Thy heavenly blessing.   Give them the Spirit of wisdom and holiness, patience and charity, zeal and watchfulness, that they may faithfully declare Thy Will, boldly rebuke vice, rightly and duly administer Thy holy Sacraments, and intercede with Thee acceptably for Thy people.   Support and comfort them under all suffering and opposition for the cause of Thy Truth, and grant that after turning many to righteousness, they may shine as the stars for ever and ever ; through JESUS CHRIST our LORD. Amen.

For Missionaries.

REMEMBER, O LORD, the Bishops well-beloved of Thee, and all others whom Thou hast called to labour among the heathen and unconverted [especially . . . .], that by them Thy Holy Name may be glorified, and Thy blessed kingdom enlarged ; through JESUS CHRIST our LORD.   Amen.

For Boys at School.

O LORD JESUS CHRIST, Who wast subject to Thine earthly superiors as a boy upon the earth; have mercy upon all who are now at school [especially . . . .], and prepare them for the work to which Thou art purposing to call them. Grant that the temptations of youth may not destroy the hopes of their mature life. Make them humble and loving, teachable and diligent. Deliver them from anger and from impurity; from dishonesty and falsehood; from sloth and fastidiousness; and from covetousness and discontent. Give them grace to set a bridle upon their fleshly desires, that they may be kept free from the bitterness of indulged sin, and, serving Thee in this world, may receive in the world to come the blessings of the pure in heart, beholding Thee with a perfect contemplation in the glory of the FATHER. Amen.

Prayer for Use in a Church.[1]

B LESS, O LORD, we beseech Thee, and prosper Thy work in this Church. Grant to the clergy who minister at Thy Altar, diligence, devotion, a right faith, and true love to those committed to their charge. Grant to those who worship here a teachable spirit, humility, charity, and steadfastness in Thy holy Faith. Supply what is wanting in Thy service and ministry, and may the offering of prayer and praise, and of Eucharistie worship abound to the glory of Thy Name and the salvation of Thy people. And grant to me, Thy unworthy servant, constant recollection, earnest devotion, and deep reverence for Thee; that, continuing faithfully in Thy service, and doing Thy holy Will, I may at last be admitted to Thy true sanctuary in Heaven, through JESUS CHRIST our LORD. Amen.

---

[1] This Prayer is suitable for use when visiting a Church.

For Unity.

O HOLY JESUS, King of the saints, and Prince of the holy Catholic Church; preserve Thy Spouse, which Thou hast purchased with Thy right hand, and redeemed and cleansed with Thy Blood, even the whole Catholic Church, from one end of the earth even to the other. Oh, preserve her safe from schism, heresy, and sacrilege. Unite all her members with the bands of faith, hope, and charity, and an external communion, when it shall seem good in Thine eyes. Let her daily sacrifice of prayer and praise, and of sacramental thanksgiving, never cease; but be for ever presented unto Thee, and for ever united to the Intercession of her dearest LORD, and for ever prevail for the obtaining for every one of her members grace and blessing, pardon and salvation. Amen.

Or this.

O GOD, the FATHER of our LORD JESUS CHRIST, our only SAVIOUR, the Prince of Peace; give us grace seriously to lay to heart the great dangers we are in by our unhappy divisions. Take away all hatred and prejudice, and whatsoever else may hinder us from godly union and concord: that as there is but one Body and one SPIRIT, and one Hope of our calling, one LORD, one Faith, one Baptism, one GOD and FATHER of us all, so we may henceforth be all of one heart, and of one soul, united in one holy bond of Truth and Peace, of Faith and Charity, and may with one mind and one mouth glorify Thee; through JESUS CHRIST our LORD. Amen.

For Visible Unity.

O LORD JESU CHRIST, Who saidst unto Thine Apostles, Peace I leave with you, My Peace I give unto you; regard not my sins, but the faith of Thy Church, and grant her that peace and unity which is agreeable to Thy Will, Who livest and reignest, GOD, for ever and ever. Amen.

Devotions for Penitence.

PRAYER BEFORE EXAMINATION OF CONSCIENCE.

✠ In the Name of the FATHER, and of the SON, and of the HOLY GHOST. Amen.

O LORD GOD, Who lightenest every man that cometh into the world, let the light of Thy grace shine into my heart, that I may search out, and discover, all my shortcomings, and my sins. Make me to see them, O LORD, as Thou seest them. Give me true contrition, that with shame and sorrow of heart I may bewail and confess those sins by which I have offended Thee. Try me, O GOD, and seek the ground of my heart ; prove me and examine my thoughts ; look well if there be any way of wickedness in me, and lead me in the way everlasting. Amen.

First Commandment.

Have I wilfully put GOD out of my thoughts ?

Have I doubted or disregarded what is declared in the Bible, or taught in the Church ?

Have I without necessity read books or kept company dangerous to the Faith ?

Have I done wrong things because others have persuaded me ?

Have I loved anyone so as to interfere with my love and duty to GOD ?

Have I despaired of mercy, or presumed on GOD's Goodness ?

Second Commandment.

Have I omitted to say my prayers every morning and evening ?

Was there ever a time when I gave up these prayers altogether? If so, how long?

Have I profaned the worship of the Church by irreverence?

Have I been irreverent at the Celebration of the Blessed Sacrament?

Have I, without necessity, omitted to kneel at the prayers?

Have I failed to bow when the Name of JESUS is mentioned in Divine Service, as the Church directs?

Have I attended places of worship contrary to the discipline of the Church?

Third Commandment.

Have I taken GOD's Name in vain by using It without thought?

Have I used His Name as a mere expression of surprise or anger?

Have I used irreverently the Names of the Sacred Persons of the Trinity?

· Have I been guilty of cursing or profane language?

Have I used holy words or spoken of sacred things in joke?

Have I made jokes about the Bible?

Have I talked lightly about the devil or hell?

Have I attended the Church Service from idle motives?

Have I said my prayers without thinking?

Have I broken promises wilfully or through carelessness?

Have I been negligent in keeping my Baptismal Vow?

Have I made a false, deceitful, or imperfect Confession?

Fourth Commandment.

Have I neglec'ed to attend the Celebration of the Blessed Sacrament on Sundays, when I had the opportunity? Have I done so on other Holy Days?

Have I stayed away from the other Divine Services without good cause?

Have I worked without necessity on Sunday?

Have I bought or sold on Sunday?

Have I spent Sunday in idle pleasure and amusements?

Have I failed to keep the Fast-days and Days of Abstinence by denying myself in food and pleasures?

Have I, in particular, neglected to observe Christmas Day, Ascension Day, Ash Wednesday, and Good Friday?

Have I received the Holy Communion when unfit or unprepared?

Have I broken GOD's law of work, by not doing my duty as well as I could, and at its proper time?

Fifth Commandment.

Have I been disobedient to my father or mother?

Have I shown rudeness to them, or to other older relations?

Have I ridiculed them?

Have I set myself against the directions or advice of the clergy?

Have I shown a want of affection to my relations?

Have I provoked, teased, or been unkind to, my brothers or sisters?

Have I been rude to servants or others who are under me?

Have I at any time grieved my parents by grave misconduct or wilful disobedience?

Have I wilfully broken the law of the land?

Have I, as a parent, teacher, or superior, neglected my duty to children or those under me?

Have I been selfish, or neglected to be of use to others?

Sixth Commandment.

Have I given way to sinful anger?

Am I easily and frequently provoked?

Have I given way to passion?

Have I injured anyone when I have been in a passion?

Have I given way to a sulky temper?

Have I been quarrelsome?

Have I been spiteful or ill-natured?

Have I refused to forgive those who have wronged or offended me?

Is there anyone against whom I have a grudge?

Have I tried to reconcile myself to those whom I have displeased?

Have I ever done acts likely to injure my life or the lives of others?

Have I been cruel to any of the lower animals? Killed or hurt them without cause?

Have I endangered the soul of anyone, by bad example, bad advice, or putting temptation in his way?

Seventh Commandment.

Have I been guilty of any act of impurity?

Have I dwelt upon impure thoughts?

Have I been guilty of talking about impure sub jects without absolute necessity?

Have I joked about impure subjects?

Have I been immodest in my person, dress, or habits?

Have I been selfish and greedy about food?

Have I indulged myself in too much drink?

Have I lain in bed too late in the morning?

Have I neglected my prayers through not getting up in time?

Have I been idle at my studies or other duties?

Have I neglected to improve my powers of body and mind?

Am I lazy in my habits?

Have I thought too much about my dress?

Have I been vain about my appearance and person?

Have I thought too highly of my talents or good qualities?

Have I forgotten that all good gifts come from GOD?

Have I neglected fasting and self-denial, according to my ability?

Eighth Commandment.

Have I stolen any money, or anything valuable?

Have I been guilty of taking little things which did not belong to me?

Have I kept things which I have found, without trying to discover the owner?

Have I taken food to which I had no right?

Have I bought or sold unfairly?

Have I cheated tradesmen, school-fellows, or other persons?

Have I passed bad money?

Have I incurred debts which I cannot pay?

Have I neglected to restore what I have stolen, or what I have gained by unfair means?

Have I neglected to give alms when I could?

Have I injured the property of others wilfully or carelessly?

Have I cheated anyone by not doing the work for which he was paying me?

Ninth Commandment.

Have I told lies so as to injure anyone?

Have I denied what I have done wrong?

Have I spoken untruly to hide my faults?

Have I told lies to save others from blame?

Have I tried to make myself appear better, or worse, than I am?

Have I practised deceitful tricks?

Have I formed a habit of telling lies?

Have I told tales against others without necessity?

Have I tried to injure the characters of others?

Have I been glad to hear, or think, or suspect, evil of others?

Tenth Commandment.

Have I been discontented with my lot in life?

Am I often guilty of grumbling?

Have I been jealous of others?

Have I given way to dislike of others who have done better than myself?

Have I been angry because I could not get what I desired?

Have I desired anything which I could not get without sin?

Have I been annoyed when others have been praised?

Have I tried to make light of the good qualities or good deeds of others?

Am I careless in doing my duty in the state of life to which I am called by GOD?

Have I made this world my chief object, instead of GOD?

Special Questions.

What is my besetting sin?

Is it growing upon me, or am I overcoming it?

Am I careless to grow in grace?

Am I living in neglect of any Means of Grace of which I should make use?

Am I neglecting any known duty?

Do I shrink back from religious duties from dislike, or fear, or shame, or laziness?

Do I put my whole trust in GOD, rely upon the merits of JESUS CHRIST only, and the grace and assistance of the HOLY SPIRIT?

Am I earnest in trying to hate and forsake sin?

Am I truly repentant for my past sins?

Am I in charity with all men?

Have I carefully performed my last penance?

Act of Confession and Contrition.

ALMIGHTY and merciful GOD, Who art of purer eyes than to behold iniquity, have mercy upon me, and look in pity on me who have sinned against Thee in thought, word, and deed. I confess to Thee all the offences which I have committed against Thee, my neighbour, and myself, especially [*here name the sins which you have discovered by your self-examination*]. For these and for all my other sins I am heartily sorry, I earnestly entreat Thy forgiveness, and I resolve, by Thy grace, to amend my life, and to serve Thee more faithfully for the time to come.

Act of Contrition.

O LORD JESU CHRIST, Very GOD and Very Man, my Creator and Redeemer, I grieve with my whole heart that I have offended Thee, my LORD and my GOD, Whom I love above all things; and I fully purpose to sin no more, to shun all occasions of sin; and in satisfaction for my sins I offer to Thee Thy most sacred Life, Thy Passion and Thy Death, and the whole price of Thy Blood which was shed for us; all my works and all my life. And I trust that of Thine infinite goodness and mercy, Thou wilt, by the merits of Thy precious Blood, forgive me all my sins; and that Thou wilt pour on me the riches of Thy Grace, whereby I may live holily, and serve Thee perfectly to the end; Who, with the FATHER and the HOLY GHOST, livest and reignest, GOD blessed for ever. Amen.

The following Devotions are for the use of those who desire to make their Confession before a Priest, according to the instructions in the Prayer-book, so as to obtain comfort and counsel, and the assurance of forgiveness.

Before Confession.

Our FATHER.

O LORD JESU CHRIST, I, a miserable sinner, desire to come unto Thee in that sacred Ordinance which Thou hast in Thy love instituted for the consolation of all sinners, that I may be washed from every stain, and cleansed from every sin, and may recover the grace which I have lost. I resolve to accuse myself, with deep humility and sorrow of heart, of all and each one of my sins, so far as I can remember them. Help me by Thy grace, and give me courage that I may confess them all to Thee, before the priest Thy minister, with true sincerity and deep penitence. And grant, gracious LORD, that, so confessing them, I may obtain that mercy and peace which Thou hast promised to all who truly repent; Who livest and reignest with the FATHER and the HOLY GHOST ever One GOD, world without end.

THE FORM OF CONFESSION.

✠ IN the Name of the FATHER, and of the SON, and of the HOLY GHOST.

I confess to GOD the FATHER Almighty, to His

Only-begotten SON JESUS CHRIST, and to GOD the HOLY GHOST, before the whole company of Heaven, and you, my father, that I have sinned exceedingly, in thought, word and deed, by my fault, by my own fault, by my own most grievous fault.

Then say—Especially I accuse myself that [since my last Confession [1]] I have sinned in [*Here say the sins which you have to confess. When you have confessed all that you remember, say*] : For these and all my other sins which I cannot now remember, I am heartily sorry, firmly purpose amendment, most humbly ask pardon of GOD ; and of you, my father, penance, counsel, and absolution.

Wherefore I pray GOD the FATHER Almighty, His Only-begotten SON JESUS CHRIST, and GOD the HOLY GHOST, to have mercy upon me, and you, my father, to pray for me to the LORD our GOD.

Here the Priest will give any necessary instruction or direction ; he will then, as he judges expedient, give Absolution.

Act of Contrition.

O LORD my GOD, I am heartily sorry for having sinned against Thee, because thereby I have offended Thee, my chief and only Good. I detest my sins, because they have displeased Thee, and I resolve, with the help of Thy grace, to avoid all occasions of sin, to bear patiently any pain or trouble that may come upon me as the punishment of sin, to make amends to those I have injured, and faithfully to perform the penance assigned to me. 'A broken and contrite heart, O God, Thou wilt not despise.'

---

[1] The words [since my last Confession] are to be omitted in a first Confession.

THANKSGIVING AFTER CONFESSION.

I GIVE Thee thanks, most merciful LORD JESUS, because Thou hast patiently waited till I, a most wretched and unworthy sinner, should return to penitence ; that Thou mightest give me pardon and forgiveness of all my sins.   Receive, I beseech Thee, this Confession which I have tried to make with humility.   Whatever has been wanting in the full and sincere confession of my sins, or in fitting sorrow for them, do Thou out of the fountain of Thy pity, and the treasury of Thy Passion, mercifully supply, and vouchsafe to have me perfectly absolved in heaven.   Grant me, LORD, the help of Thy grace, that henceforth I may avoid sin, and more faithfully serve Thee.   I have sworn, and am steadfastly purposed to keep Thy righteous judgments, by Thy help, Who, with the FATHER and the HOLY GHOST, livest and reignest, One GOD, world without end.   Amen.

PIOUS AFFECTIONS OF THE SOUL.

For benefits received in Confession.

PRAISE the LORD, O my soul : and all that is within me, praise His Holy Name.

Praise the LORD, O my soul : and forget not all His benefits.

Who forgiveth all thy sin : and healeth all thine infirmities.

Who saveth thy life from destruction : and crowneth thee with mercy and loving-kindness.

Who satisfieth thy mouth with good things : making thee young and lusty as an eagle.

He hath not dealt with us after our sins : nor rewarded us after our iniquities.

For look how high the heaven is in comparison of

the earth : so great is His mercy towards them that fear Him.

Look how wide also the east is from the west : ' so far hath He set our sins from us.

Yea, like as a father pitieth his own children : even so is the LORD merciful unto them that fear Him.

Our FATHER.

O SAVIOUR of the world, Who by Thy Cross and precious Blood hast redeemed us, save us and help us, we humbly beseech Thee, O LORD. Amen.

ASPIRATIONS BEFORE OR AFTER CONFESSION.

MY LORD and my GOD, I sincerely acknowledge myself a vile and wretched sinner, unworthy to appear in Thy presence ; but do Thou have mercy on me, and save me.

Most loving FATHER, I have sinned against heaven and before Thee, and am unworthy to be called Thy child ; make me as one of Thy servants, and may I for the future be ever faithful to Thee.

It truly grieves me, O my GOD, to have sinned, and so many times transgressed Thy law ; but wash me now from my iniquity, and cleanse me from my sin. O loving FATHER, assist me by Thy grace, that I may bring forth worthy fruits of penance.

Oh, that I had never transgressed Thy commandments ! Oh, that I had never sinned ! Happy those souls who have preserved their innocence : oh, that I had been so happy !

But now I am resolved, with the help of Thy grace, to be more watchful over myself, to amend my failings, and fulfil Thy law. Look down on me with the eyes of mercy, O GOD, and blot out my sins.

Forgive me what is past, and through Thine infinite goodness, secure me, by Thy grace, against all my wonted failings for the time to come.

Thou didst come, O dear REDEEMER, not to call the righteous, but sinners to repentance ; behold a miserable sinner here before Thee : oh, draw me powerfully to Thyself.

Have mercy upon me, O GOD, after Thy great goodness : according to the multitude of Thy mercies, do away my offences. Wash me with Thy precious Blood, and I shall be whiter than snow.

How great is Thy goodness, O LORD, in having so long spared such a worthless servant, and waited with so much patience for his amendment ! What return shall I make for Thy infinite mercies? Oh, let this mercy be added to the rest, that I may never more offend Thee: this favour I earnestly beg of Thee, O LORD, that I may now for the future renounce my own way to follow Thine. Help me, O LORD JESU, and have compassion on my sinful soul, for Thy mercy's sake. Amen.

A PRAYER FOR THE GRACE OF TRUE REPENTANCE.

O LORD my GOD, give me, I pray Thee, the spirit of true repentance, and take away from me all that separates me from Thee, and makes me unworthy of Thy love. Assist me by Thy grace to gain a deeper sorrow for my sins, and to form more sincere resolutions to amend my life. I have wearied Thee, yet turn again once more and seek Thy servant, and I shall live. O my GOD, have mercy upon me and succour me with Thy gracious help. Create in me a clean heart and renew a right spirit within me, and give me grace to renounce my sins and the occasions of them, diligently to keep my good resolutions, and obtain of Thee deliverance from all my offences ; through JESUS CHRIST our LORD and SAVIOUR. Amen.

The Blessed Sacrament.

A SHORT FORM OF PREPARATION FOR COMMUNION.

One of the following Prayers may be added to the usual Morning and Evening Prayers during the week before Communion ; or for two or three days, in the case of frequent Communicants.

I.

O BLESSED JESUS, Who dost vouchsafe to come even to us Thy unworthy servants in the Blessed Sacrament of Thy Body and Blood, prepare me, I humbly beseech Thee, to receive Thee for the strengthening and refreshing of my soul. Give me true repentance for my past sins, grace humbly to confess them, true faith in Thee Who didst die on the Cross to save me, a firm purpose to keep from all that displeases Thee, and charity to forgive all who have wronged or vexed me.

LORD, come to me that Thou mayest cleanse me.
LORD, come to me that Thou mayest heal me.
LORD, come to me that Thou mayest strengthen me.
And grant that, having received Thee, I may not forget Thee, or drive Thee from my soul by being careless about pleasing Thee, but may continue Thine for ever. Amen.

II.

O LORD JESUS CHRIST, Who hast vouchsafed to provide Thy Body and Blood for food and drink unto Thy servants, in the offering and re-

ception whereof Thou willest to recall the memory of
Thy Passion and Death : give me grace that in per-
forming this Thy most holy Will, I may be able to
receive the abundant fruits of Thy Sacrament ; Who
livest and reignest with the FATHER and the HOLY
GHOST, One GOD, world without end.   Amen.

III.

(*From S. Thomas Aquinas.*)

ALMIGHTY, Everlasting GOD, lo! I approach
to the Sacrament of Thy Only-Begotten Son,
our LORD JESUS CHRIST ; I approach sick to the
Physician of life, unclean to the Fountain of mercy,
blind to the Light of eternal brightness, poor and
needy to the Lord of heaven and earth ; I pray Thee,
therefore, of the abundance of Thy boundless bounty,
that Thou wouldest vouchsafe to heal my sickness, to
wash my defilements, to enlighten my blindness, to
enrich my poverty, to clothe my nakedness; that I
may receive the Bread of Angels, the King of Kings
and Lord of Lords, with such reverence and humility,
such contrition and devotion, such purity and faith,
as is expedient for the health of my soul.   Grant, I
beseech Thee, that I may receive not only the Sacrament of the Body and Blood of the LORD, but the
Substance also, and virtue of the Sacrament.   O most
gracious GOD, grant me so to receive the Body of
Thy Only-Begotten Son, our LORD JESUS CHRIST,
which He took of the Virgin Mary, that I may be
found worthy to be incorporated into His Mystical Body,
and accounted among His members.   O most loving
FATHER, grant that I may at length behold with unveiled face Thy beloved SON, Whom now I purpose to
receive veiled in my pilgrimage, Who, with Thee,
liveth and reigneth in the Unity of the HOLY GHOST,
One GOD, throughout all ages.   Amen.

Psalms 84, 85, 86 or 130 may be added.

DIRECTION OF THE INTENTION.[1]

O LORD JESU CHRIST, Who didst vouchsafe to offer up Thyself on the Altar of the Cross as the full, perfect, and sufficient Sacrifice for the sins of the whole world, and didst ordain Thy Blessed Sacrament as a Memorial for ever of that most precious Sacrifice, I desire to assist at the Celebration of these sacred Mysteries [2 and to receive Thy most holy Body and Blood], beseeching Thee to bestow upon me therein the fulness of Thy blessing, and especially to grant me [*here say what especial object you intend to pray for at the Celebration*], and all that Thou seest expedient for my body and soul, and for my salvation. Grant this, I pray Thee, for Thine infinite merits, Who livest and reignest with the FATHER and the HOLY GHOST, ever One GOD, world without end. Amen.

The most important and necessary part of Preparation for Holy Communion consists in Self-examination. Devotions and Forms for this are provided at page 47. It is recommended that those who intend to communicate should one or two days previously take an opportunity of using this, or some other, method of Self-examination, following it with humble confession, and such Prayers of Preparation as they find suitable. And those who have scruples or difficulties, or who are troubled by grievous sins, are exhorted to make their Confession to a Priest, according to the Instructions on page 54.

---

[1] It is recommended that some special favour should be asked of GOD at each celebration of the Holy Communion- *e.g.* some blessing to our friends or ourselves.

[2] To be said by those who intend actually to communicate.

✠

THE ORDER OF THE

ADMINISTRATION OF THE LORD'S SUPPER,

OR,

HOLY COMMUNION.

Before the Service.

✠ In the Name of the Father, and of the Son, and of the Holy Ghost.   Amen.

O ALMIGHTY FATHER, behold I, an un-worthy sinner, presume to appear before Thee to assist in offering up to Thee the Sacrifice of the Body and Blood of Thy SON JESUS CHRIST, in union with that Sacrifice which He offered to Thee once upon the Cross : (1) for Thine own honour, praise, adoration and glory ; (2) in thankful remembrance of His Death and Passion ; (3) in thanksgiving for all Thy blessings bestowed upon me and upon Thy Church, [especially . . .] ; (4) for obtaining pardon and remission of all my sins [especially . . .] ; (5) for my own salvation and the salvation of [. . .] ; and (6) for the consolation of those who are departed in Thy faith and fear [especially . . .].

O merciful GOD, be Thou pleased so to aid me by Thy grace, that I may behave myself as I ought to do in Thy Divine Presence, and that I may so com-memorate the Death and Passion of Thy blessed SON ['and so receive his most blessed Body and Blood], as to partake most fully of the fruits thereof ; through the same JESUS CHRIST our LORD.

' To be said by those who are actually intending to com-municate.

Prayer for the Priest.

RECEIVE, O LORD, this Sacrifice at the hands of Thy priest, to Thy greater glory and the benefit of our souls, Who livest and reignest, One GOD, world without end.

OUR FATHER Which art in heaven, Hallowed be Thy Name. Thy kingdom come. Thy Will be done in earth, As it is in heaven. Give us this day our daily bread. And forgive us our trespasses, As we forgive them that trespass against us. And lead us not into temptation ; But deliver us from evil. Amen.

The Collect for Purity.

ALMIGHTY GOD, unto Whom all hearts be open, all desires known, and from Whom no secrets are hid ; Cleanse the thoughts of our hearts by the inspiration of Thy HOLY SPIRIT, that we may perfectly love Thee, and worthily magnify Thy Holy Name ; through CHRIST our LORD. *Amen.*

THE COMMANDMENTS.

GOD spake these words and said ; I am the LORD thy GOD ; thou shalt have none other gods but Me.

People. LORD, have mercy upon us, and incline our hearts to keep this law.

Minister. Thou shalt not make to thyself any graven image, nor the likeness of any thing that is in heaven above, or in the earth beneath, or in the water under the earth. Thou shalt not bow down to them, nor worship them : for I the LORD thy GOD am a jealous GOD, and visit the sins of the fathers upon the children, unto the third and fourth generation of them that hate Me, and shew mercy unto thousands in them that love Me, and keep My commandments.

People. LORD, have mercy upon us, and incline our hearts to keep this law.

Minister. Thou shalt not take the Name of the LORD thy GOD in vain : for the LORD will not hold him guiltless, that taketh His Name in vain.

People. LORD, have mercy upon us, and incline our hearts to keep this law.

Minister. Remember that thou keep holy the Sabbath-day. Six days shalt thou labour, and do all that thou hast to do ; but the seventh day is the Sabbath of the LORD thy GOD. In it thou shalt do no manner of work, thou, and thy son, and thy daughter, thy man-servant, and thy maid-servant, thy cattle, and the stranger that is within thy gates. For in six days the LORD made heaven and earth, the sea, and all that in them is, and rested the seventh day : wherefore the LORD blessed the seventh day, and hallowed it.

People. LORD, have mercy upon us, and incline our hearts to keep this law.

Minister. Honour thy father and thy mother ; that thy days may be long in the land, which the LORD thy GOD giveth thee.

People. LORD, have mercy upon us, and incline our hearts to keep this law.

Minister. Thou shalt do no murder.

People. LORD, have mercy upon us, and incline our hearts to keep this law.

Minister. Thou shalt not commit adultery.

People. LORD, have mercy upon us, and incline our hearts to keep this law.

Minister. Thou shalt not steal.

People. LORD, have mercy upon us, and incline our hearts to keep this law.

Minister. Thou shalt not bear false witness against thy neighbour.

People. LORD, have mercy upon us, and incline our hearts to keep this law.

Minister. Thou shalt not covet thy neighbour's house, thou shalt not covet thy neighbour's wife, nor his servant, nor his maid, nor his ox, nor his ass, nor anything that is his.

People. LORD, have mercy upon us, and

F

write all these Thy laws in our hearts, we beseech Thee.

THE PRAYER FOR THE QUEEN.

Let us pray.

ALMIGHTY GOD, Whose kingdom is everlasting, and power infinite ; Have mercy upon the whole Church ; and so rule the heart of Thy chosen Servant *VICTORIA*, our Queen and Governour, that she (knowing whose minister she is) may above all things seek Thy honour and glory : and that we, and all her subjects (duly considering whose authority she hath) may faithfully serve, honour, and humbly obey her, in Thee, and for Thee, according to Thy blessed Word and ordinance ; through JESUS CHRIST our LORD, Who with Thee and the HOLY GHOST liveth and reigneth, ever one GOD, world without end. *Amen.*

Or,

ALMIGHTY and Everlasting GOD, we are taught by Thy holy Word, that the hearts of kings are in Thy rule and governance, and that Thou dost dispose and turn them as it seemeth best to Thy godly wisdom : We humbly beseech Thee so to dispose and govern the heart *VICTORIA* Thy Servant, our Queen and

Governour, that, in all her thoughts, words, and works, she may ever seek Thy honour and glory, and study to preserve Thy people committed to her charge, in wealth, peace, and godliness: Grant this, O merciful Father, for Thy dear Son's sake, JESUS CHRIST our LORD. *Amen.*

THE COLLECT FOR THE DAY.

THE EPISTLE.

THE HOLY GOSPEL.

Before the Gospel.
Glory be to Thee, O LORD.

After the Gospel.
Praise be to Thee, O CHRIST.

Or,
Thanks be to Thee, O LORD.

THE NICENE CREED.

I BELIEVE in one GOD the FATHER Almighty, Maker of heaven and earth, And of all things visible and invisible:

And in One LORD JESUS CHRIST, the Only-Begotten SON of GOD, Begotten of His Father before all worlds, GOD of GOD, Light of Light, Very GOD of Very GOD, Begotten, not made, Being of one Substance with the FATHER; By

Whom all things were made ; Who for us men, and for our salvation came down from Heaven, AND WAS INCARNATE BY THE HOLY GHOST OF THE VIRGIN MARY, AND WAS MADE MAN. And was crucified also for us under Pontius Pilate. He suffered and was buried ; And the third day He rose again according to the Scriptures ; And ascended into heaven, And sitteth on the right hand of the FATHER. And He shall come again with glory to judge both the quick and the dead : Whose Kingdom shall have no end.

And I believe in the HOLY GHOST, The LORD, and Giver of life, Who proceedeth from the FATHER and the SON ; Who with the FATHER and the SON together is worshipped and glorified, Who spake by the Prophets. And I believe One Catholick and Apostolick Church. I acknowledge One Baptism for the remission of sins, And I look for the Resurrection of the dead, And the life of the world to come. *Amen.*

THE OFFERTORY.

LET your light so shine before men, that they may see your good works, and glorify your Father which is in heaven.—*S. Matt.* v. 16.

At the Offering of Alms.

WHO am I, that I should be able to offer so willingly after this sort ? For all things come of Thee, O LORD, and of Thine own have we given Thee.

At the Oblation of the Elements.

RECEIVE, O Holy TRINITY, this Oblation, which I join in offering unto Thee in memory of the Passion of our LORD JESUS CHRIST, and grant that it may be acceptable in Thy sight, and promote my salvation, and that of all Thy faithful people, both living and departed, through JESUS CHRIST our LORD. Amen.

Acts of the Principal Virtues.

Thanks.—O LORD JESU, what great things hast Thou done, and what didst Thou suffer, out of the power of Thy boundless love to me ! But what return have I made ? and what return shall I make ?

Contrition.—I am sorry from the bottom of my heart, that I have ever offended Thee, Who hast so greatly loved me.

Faith.—I believe in Thee with a lively faith, O Eternal Truth; because Thou art Thyself GOD and Man, my LORD and SAVIOUR.

Hope.—I hope in Thee, O LORD, O only Hope, and true salvation of my soul.

Charity.—I love Thee, O my sovereign Good ! Oh, that I may love Thee above all things with my whole heart ! Oh, may the burning power of Thy love

absorb me, that nothing may ever separate me from
Thee, my SAVIOUR! For whom have I in heaven
but Thee? and there is none upon earth that I desire
in comparison of Thee.

THE PRAYER FOR THE CHURCH.

Let us pray for the whole state of CHRIST'S
Church militant here in earth.

ALMIGHTY and Everliving GOD, Who by
Thy holy Apostle hast taught us to make
prayers and supplications, and to give thanks,
for all men : We humbly beseech Thee most
mercifully to accept our Alms and Oblations, and
to receive these our prayers, which we offer unto
Thy Divine Majesty ; beseeching Thee to inspire continually the Universal Church with the
SPIRIT of truth, unity, and concord : And grant,
that all they that do confess Thy holy Name
may agree in the truth of Thy holy Word, and
live in unity, and godly love.

We beseech Thee also to save and defend
all Christian Kings, Princes, and Governours ;
and specially Thy Servant *VICTORIA* our
Queen : that under her we may be godly and
quietly governed : And grant unto her whole
Council, and to all that are put in authority
under her, that they may truly and indifferently
minister justice, to the punishment of wickedness

and vice, and to the maintenance of Thy true religion, and virtue.

Give grace, O Heavenly FATHER, to all Bishops and Curates, that they may both by their life and doctrine set forth Thy true and lively Word, and rightly and duly administer Thy Holy Sacraments :

And to all Thy people give Thy heavenly grace ; and especially to this congregation here present ; that with meek heart and due reverence, they may hear, and receive Thy holy Word ; truly serving Thee in holiness and righteousness all the days of their life.

And we most humbly beseech Thee of Thy goodness, O LORD, to comfort and succour all them, who in this transitory life are in trouble, sorrow, need, sickness, or any other adversity.

And we also bless Thy holy Name for all Thy servants departed this life in Thy faith and fear ; beseeching Thee to give us grace so to follow their good examples, that with them we may be partakers of Thy heavenly Kingdom :

Grant this, O FATHER, for JESUS CHRIST'S sake, our only Mediator and Advocate. *Amen.*

THE INVITATION.

YE that do truly and earnestly repent you of your sins, and are in love and charity with your neighbours, and intend to lead a new life, following the commandments of GOD, and walking from henceforth in His holy ways; Draw near with faith, and take this holy Sacrament to your comfort; and make your humble confession to Almighty GOD, meekly kneeling upon your knees.

THE GENERAL CONFESSION.

ALMIGHTY GOD, FATHER of our LORD JESUS CHRIST, Maker of all things, Judge of all men; We acknowledge and bewail our manifold sins and wickedness, Which we, from time to time, most grievously have committed, By thought, word, and deed, Against Thy Divine Majesty, Provoking most justly Thy wrath and indignation against us. We do earnestly repent, And are heartily sorry for these our misdoings; The remembrance of them is grievous unto us; The burden of them is intolerable. Have mercy upon us, Have mercy upon us, most merciful FATHER; For Thy SON our LORD JESUS CHRIST'S sake, Forgive us all that is past; And grant that we may ever hereafter Serve and please Thee, In newness of life, To the honour and glory of Thy Name; through JESUS CHRIST our LORD. *Amen.*

THE ABSOLUTION.

ALMIGHTY GOD, our heavenly FATHER, Who of His great mercy hath promised forgiveness of sins to all them that with hearty repentance and true faith turn unto Him ; Have mercy upon you ; pardon and deliver you from all your sins ; confirm and strengthen you in all goodness ; and bring you to everlasting life ; through JESUS CHRIST our LORD. Amen.

THE COMFORTABLE WORDS.

Hear what comfortable words our SAVIOUR CHRIST saith unto all that truly turn to Him.

COME unto Me all that travail and are heavy laden, and I will refresh you.—*S. Matt.* xi. 28.

GOD so loved the world, that He gave His only-begotten Son, to the end that all that believe in Him should not perish, but have everlasting life.—*St. John* iii. 16.

Hear also what Saint Paul saith.

This is a true saying, and worthy of all men to be received, That CHRIST JESUS came into the world to save sinners.—1 *Tim.* i. 15.

Hear also what Saint John saith.

If any man sin, we have an Advocate with the FATHER, JESUS CHRIST the Righteous ; and He is the Propitiation for our sins.—1 *S. John* ii. 1.

THE SURSUM CORDA.

Priest. Lift up your hearts.

Answer. We lift them up unto the LORD.

Priest. Let us give thanks unto our LORD GOD.

Answer. It is meet and right so to do.

THE PREFACE.

IT is very meet, right, and our bounden duty, that we should at all times, and in all places, give thanks unto Thee, O LORD, [HOLY FATHER,[1]] Almighty, Everlasting God.

[*Here, on certain great days, a proper Preface is inserted.*[2]]

THEREFORE with Angels and Archangels, and with all the company of heaven, we laud and magnify Thy glorious Name ; evermore praising Thee, and saying,

THE SANCTUS.

HOLY, Holy, Holy, LORD GOD of Hosts, Heaven and earth are full of Thy glory : Glory be to Thee, O LORD most High. *Amen.*

THE PRAYER OF HUMBLE ACCESS.

WE do not presume to come to this Thy Table, O merciful LORD, trusting in our

---

[1] The words [HOLY FATHER] must be omitted on Trinity Sunday.

[2] For the proper Prefaces, see p. 85.

own righteousness, but in Thy manifold and great mercies. We are not worthy so much as to gather up the crumbs under Thy Table. But Thou art the same LORD, Whose property is always to have mercy: Grant us, therefore, gracious LORD, so to eat the Flesh of Thy dear Son JESUS CHRIST, and to drink His Blood, that our sinful bodies may be made clean by His Body, and our souls washed through His most precious Blood, and that we may evermore dwell in Him, and He in us. *Amen.*

HAVE mercy upon us, O LORD our GOD, after Thy great mercy, and send down and upon these gifts lying before Thee, Thy HOLY SPIRIT, that He may make this bread the Holy Body, and this cup the Blood of Thy CHRIST; that It may be to us who partake of It for the remission of sins, and for the sanctification of soul and body unto life everlasting. Amen.

BLESSED is He that cometh in the Name of the LORD, Hosanna in the Highest.

THE CONSECRATION.

ALMIGHTY GOD, our Heavenly FATHER, Who of Thy tender mercy didst give Thine Only Son JESUS CHRIST to suffer death upon the Cross for our Redemption, Who made there, by His one Oblation of Himself once offered, a full, perfect, and sufficient Sacrifice, Oblation, and Satisfaction, for the sins of the whole world ; and did institute, and in His Holy Gospel command us to continue a perpetual Memory of that His precious Death, until His coming again ;

Hear us, O merciful FATHER, we most humbly beseech Thee ; and grant, that we receiving these Thy creatures of Bread and Wine, according to Thy Son our SAVIOUR JESUS CHRIST'S holy institution, in remembrance of His Death and Passion, may be partakers of His most Blessed Body and Blood :

THE INVOCATION.

Who in the same night that He was betrayed, took Bread, and when He had given thanks, He brake It, and gave It to His disciples, saying, Take, Eat, THIS IS MY BODY WHICH IS GIVEN FOR YOU : Do this in Remembrance of Me.

CONSECRATION OF THE BREAD.

Likewise after Supper He took the Cup ; and when He had given thanks, He gave It to them, saying : Drink ye all of this ; FOR THIS IS MY BLOOD OF THE NEW TESTAMENT, WHICH IS SHED FOR YOU AND FOR MANY FOR THE REMISSION OF SINS : Do This as oft as ye shall drink It, in remembrance of Me.   Amen.

CONSECRATION OF THE CUP.

✠

After the Consecration.

I ADORE Thee, O LORD my GOD, veiled under these poor earthly Elements Prostrate before Thy Divine Majesty, I desire to honour Thee with all the devotion of which I am capable; and that I may the better honour Thee, I unite myself with all Thy Saints and Angels in their more perfect adoration.

Hail! Living Bread, that comest down from heaven to give life to the world! Hail, most Heavenly Drink of JESUS' Blood! to me above all things the sum and fulness of delight; my soul blesses Thee for Thy love, thus deigning to remain hidden for our salvation under these Forms of Thy creatures.

May my life be hidden with Thee in GOD, that, dying to myself, I may live only to Thee, praising and magnifying Thee, till I behold Thee unveiled, to be adored face to face, through all eternity! Amen.

Agnus Dei.

O Lamb of GOD : That takest away the sins of the world ;
Have mercy upon us.
O Lamb of GOD : That takest away the sins of the world ;
Have mercy upon us.
O Lamb of GOD : That takest away the sins of the world ;
Grant us Thy peace.

Act of Intercession.

O ALMIGHTY FATHER, I offer to Thee this Sacrifice in union with the perpetual Intercession of Thy SON our LORD, for the whole world ; that they who know Thee not may be brought to the knowledge and love of Thy Truth ; for Thy Church, that it may be filled with the fruits of Thy Righteousness; for all who are in wilful sin or error, that they may be converted unto Thee; for all Thy faithful, now struggling through trial, in weakness or in any suffering, spiritual or bodily, that they may be sustained, and increase in Thy manifold gifts of grace; and for all those on whose behalf I am bound or accustomed to pray [especially . . .], I offer It also for the souls of those who have departed this life with the seal of faith [especially . . .], that Thou mayst grant them perpetual light and perfect purification.

Have mercy upon all sinners, and in Thine own good time unite all Thy people in One Faith and Love. Amen.

Act of Spiritual Communion.[1]

O MY JESU! my most loving SAVIOUR, Sweetness of Divine Love! Spouse of holy souls! Come, I pray Thee, within my soul; pervade all my substance, and flow even through all my faculties of soul and body, that I may be dissolved in blissful union with Thee.

Even though I cannot now receive Thee sacramentally, yet come spiritually within my soul, and pardon and remove utterly from me the sins, infirmities, or hindrances which prevent my approaching nearer Thee.

Oh, possess me wholly; let the consuming fire of Thy love absorb me, and unite me so closely with Thyself, that it may be no longer I that live, but Thou who livest in me.

Come Thou Life of my soul, rule me and every movement of my being with an absolute dominion, that I being made one with Thee, and Thou with me, every hurtful desire and affection may be quenched in me, and every virtue may be matured in me after Thy likeness. Amen.

---

[1] To be said by those not actually communicating.

FOR COMMUNICANTS.

Before receiving the Paten.

I will take the Bread of heaven, and call upon the Name of the LORD. LORD, I am not worthy that Thou shouldest come under my roof; but speak the word only, and my soul shall be healed.

When the Priest delivers the Blessed Sacrament of our Lord's Body, he says,

THE BODY of our LORD JESUS CHRIST, which was given for thee, preserve thy body and soul unto everlasting life. (*Amen.*) Take and eat This in remembrance that CHRIST died for thee, and feed on Him in thy heart by faith with thanksgiving.

O my GOD, Thou art holy: O my soul, thou art blessed.

Before receiving the Chalice.

What reward shall I give unto the LORD for all the benefits that He hath done unto me? I will receive the Cup of Salvation, and will call upon the Name of the LORD.

When the Priest delivers the Blessed Sacrament of our Lord's Blood, he says,

THE BLOOD of our LORD JESUS CHRIST, which was shed for thee, preserve thy body and soul unto everlasting life. (*Amen.*) Drink This in remembrance that CHRIST'S BLOOD was shed for thee, and be thankful.

Let my sins be washed away in Thy Blood, O LORD.

Then think of the special favour [1] *you intend to ask from God and say,*

O ETERNAL FATHER, I receive this Blessed Sacrament, humbly beseeching Thee through It to grant me [. . .] for the sake of Him Who now dwelleth in me. Amen.

On returning from the Altar.

THANKS be unto GOD for His unspeakable Gift! I have found Him Whom my soul loveth; I will hold Him and not let Him go.

(*The Nunc Dimittis and the Te Deum may be added.*)

THANKSGIVING AFTER COMMUNICATING.

I YIELD Thee thanks, O LORD, Holy FATHER, Almighty Everlasting GOD, Who hast refreshed me with the most holy Body and Blood of Thy Son our LORD JESUS CHRIST. And I pray that this Sacrament of our Salvation, which I, an unworthy sinner, have received, may not come into judgment or condemnation against me according to my deserts, but may be for the advancement of my soul and body to life eternal. Amen.

O LORD JESUS CHRIST, be merciful to me, and by Thy Body and Blood, which I have now received, cleanse me from all my sins. For Thou hast said, Whoso eateth My Flesh and drinketh My Blood dwelleth in Me and I in Him. Wherefore I humbly pray Thee to make me a clean heart and to renew a right spirit within me, to deliver me from all the snares of the devil, and cleanse me from all my faults [especially . . .], that so I may be partaker of Thy heavenly joys; Who livest and reignest with the FATHER and the HOLY GHOST, ever one GOD, world without end. Amen.

---

[1] See page 61.

ANIMA CHRISTI.

SOUL of CHRIST, sanctify me ;
Body of CHRIST, save me ;
Blood of CHRIST, refresh me ;
Water from the Side of CHRIST, cleanse me ;
Passion of CHRIST, strengthen me ;
O good JESU, hear me ;
Within Thy Wounds hide me ;
Suffer me not to be separated from Thee ;
From the malicious enemy defend me ;
In the hour of my death call me ;
And bid me come to Thee,
That with Thy saints I may praise Thee,
For ever and ever.   Amen.

Additional prayers for Communion will be found
on p. III.

OUR FATHER, Which art in heaven, Hallowed be Thy Name. Thy kingdom come.   Thy will be done in earth, As it is in heaven.   Give us this day our daily bread. And forgive us our trespasses, As we forgive them that trespass against us.   And lead us not into temptation ; But deliver us from evil: For Thine is the kingdom, The power, and the glory, For ever and ever.   Amen.

PRAYER OF OBLATION.

O LORD and Heavenly FATHER, we Thy humble servants entirely desire Thy
THE   Fatherly Goodness mercifully to
OBLATION.   accept This our Sacrifice of Praise
and thanksgiving ;

G

Most humbly beseeching Thee to grant, that by the merits and death of Thy SON JESUS CHRIST, and through faith in His Blood, we and all Thy whole Church may obtain remission of our sins, and all other benefits of His Passion.

And here we offer and present unto Thee, O LORD, ourselves, our souls, and bodies, to be a reasonable, holy, THE OBLATION OF OURSELVES. and living sacrifice unto Thee; humbly beseeching Thee, that all we, who are partakers of this Holy Communion, may be fulfilled with Thy grace and heavenly benediction.

And although we be unworthy, through our manifold sins, to offer unto Thee any sacrifice, yet we beseech Thee to accept This our bounden duty and service; not weighing our merits, but pardoning our offences, through JESUS CHRIST our LORD;

By Whom, and with Whom, in the Unity of the HOLY GHOST, all honour and glory be unto Thee, O FATHER Almighty, world without end. *Amen.*

Or this.

ALMIGHTY and Everliving GOD, we most heartily thank Thee, for that Thou dost vouchsafe to feed us, who have duly received these holy Mysteries, with the spiritual food of the most precious Body and Blood of Thy SON our SAVIOUR JESUS CHRIST ; and dost assure us thereby of Thy favour and goodness towards us ; and that we are very members incorporate in the mystical body of Thy SON, which is the blessed company of all faithful people ; and are also heirs through hope of Thy everlasting kingdom, by the merits of the most precious Death and Passion of Thy dear SON. And we most humbly beseech Thee, O Heavenly FATHER, so to assist us with Thy grace, that we may continue in that holy fellowship, and do all such good works as Thou hast prepared for us to walk in ; through JESUS CHRIST our LORD, to Whom with Thee and the HOLY GHOST be all honour and glory, world without end. *Amen.*

THE GLORIA IN EXCELSIS.

GLORY be to GOD on high, and in earth peace, good will towards men. We praise Thee, we bless Thee, we worship Thee, we glorify Thee, we give thanks to Thee for Thy great glory, O LORD GOD, heavenly King, GOD the FATHER Almighty.

O LORD, the Only-Begotten Son JESU CHRIST ; O LORD GOD, Lamb of GOD, SON of the FATHER, that takest away the sins of the world, have mercy upon us. Thou that takest away the sins of the world, have mercy upon us. Thou that takest away the sins of the world, receive

our prayer.   Thou that sittest at the right hand
of GOD the FATHER, have mercy upon us.

For Thou only art holy ; Thou only art the
LORD ; Thou only, O CHRIST, with the HOLY
GHOST, art most high in the glory of GOD the
FATHER. *Amen.*

THE BLESSING.

THE Peace of GOD, which passeth all understanding, keep your hearts and minds in
the Knowledge and Love of GOD,   THE PEACE.
and of His SON JESUS CHRIST our LORD ;

And the Blessing of GOD Almighty, the
FATHER, the SON, and the HOLY   THE BLESSING.
GHOST, be amongst you and remain with you
always. *Amen.*

After the Blessing.

ALMIGHTY and everlasting GOD, the Preserver
of souls and the Redeemer of the world ;
graciously behold me Thy servant, who humble myself before Thy Divine Majesty. Accept this Sacrifice,
which to the honour of Thy Name we have offered
for the faithful living and departed, and for all our
sins and offences.   Take away Thine anger from us :
open unto us the gates of Paradise ; deliver us by Thy
power from all evils, and whatever faults and failings
have taken hold upon us during this holy service, do
Thou forgive.   And grant that we may so persevere
in Thy precepts unto the end, that we may be made
worthy to be joined to the company of Thine elect, by
Thy power, O my GOD, Whose blessed Name, Honour,
and Dominion, shall endure for ever and ever. Amen.

PROPER PREFACES.

Upon Christmas-day, *and seven days after.*

BECAUSE Thou didst give JESUS CHRIST Thine only SON to be born as at this time for us; Who, by the operation of the HOLY GHOST, was made Very Man of the substance of the Virgin Mary His mother; and that without spot of sin, to make us clean from all sin. Therefore with Angels, &c.

Upon Easter-day *and seven days after.*

BUT chiefly are we bound to praise Thee for the glorious Resurrection of Thy SON JESUS CHRIST our LORD; for He is the very Paschal Lamb, which was offered for us, and hath taken away the sin of the world; Who by His death hath destroyed death, and by His rising to life again hath restored to us everlasting life. Therefore with Angels, &c.

Upon Ascension-day, *and seven days after.*

THROUGH Thy most dearly beloved SON JESUS CHRIST our LORD; Who after His most glorious Resurrection manifestly appeared to all His Apostles, and in their sight ascended up into heaven to prepare a place for us; that where He is, thither we might also ascend, and reign with Him in glory. Therefore with Angels, &c.

Upon Whitsun-day, *and six days after.*

THROUGH JESUS CHRIST our LORD; according to Whose most true promise, the HOLY GHOST came down as at this time from heaven with a sudden great sound, as it had been a mighty wind, in the likeness of fiery tongues, lighting upon the Apostles, to teach them, and to lead them to all truth ; giving them both the gift of divers languages, and also boldness with fervent zeal constantly to preach the Gospel unto all nations ; whereby we have been brought out of darkness and error into the clear light and true knowledge of Thee, and of Thy SON JESUS CHRIST.   Therefore with Angels, &c.

Upon the Feast of Trinity *only.*

WHO art One GOD, One LORD ; not One only Person, but Three Persons in One Substance.   For that which we believe of the glory of the FATHER, the same we believe of the SON, and of the HOLY GHOST, without any difference or inequality.   Therefore with Angels, &c.

THANKSGIVINGS AFTER HOLY COMMUNION.

One of these may be added to the usual Morning and Evening Prayers, for two days after Communion.

I.

I THANK Thee, O LORD GOD Almighty, for the blessing which Thou hast vouchsafed me, in admitting me to partake of Thy holy, precious, and heavenly Mysteries ; and I beseech Thee to grant that through the Communion of the holy Body and Blood of Thy dear SON, we may increase in holiness of heart and life, and be hereafter made partakers of eternal glory with Him, Who liveth and reigneth with Thee and the HOLY GHOST, ever One GOD, world without end. Amen.

II.

(From Bishop Andrewes.)

GRANT, O LORD JESU, that I may henceforth faithfully follow and serve Thee, Who hast at this time so lovingly vouchsafed to come to me ; and because, through my infirmities, I cannot follow Thee as I would, be pleased to assist me with Thy Power, and draw me after Thee. May my soul be so strengthened by virtue of this Sacrament, that it may esteem nothing pleasing or delightful in comparison of Thee, that it may lust after no transitory thing, nor be disquieted with any worldly cross ; but grant that by Thy assisting grace I may overcome all the trials and temptations of this life, and may bless Thee for ever in the world to come, Who livest and reignest with the FATHER and the HOLY GHOST, One GOD, world without end. Amen.

III.

(From St. Thomas Aquinas.)

I YIELD Thee thanks, O LORD, Holy FATHER, Almighty, Everlasting GOD, Who hast vouchsafed, not for any merit of mine, but only out of the condescension of Thy Mercy, to feed me, a sinner, Thy unworthy servaut, with the precious Body and Blood of Thy SON our LORD JESUS CHRIST. And I pray that this Holy Communion may not bring guilt upon me to condemnation, but may intercede for me to my pardon and salvation. Let it be to me an armour of faith, and a shield of good resolution ; a riddance of all vices ; an extermination of evil desires and longings ; an increase of love and patience, of humility and obedience, and all virtues ; a firm defence against the wiles of my enemies, visible and invisible ; a perfect quieting of all my impulses, fleshly and spiritual ; a firm adherence to Thee, the One True GOD, and a blessed consummation of my end ; and I pray Thee that Thou wouldest vouchsafe to bring me, a sinner, to that ineffable Feast, where Thou, with Thy SON, and the HOLY SPIRIT, are to Thy holy ones' true Light, full Satiety, everlasting Joy, Pleasure consummated, and perfect Happiness ; through the same our LORD JESUS CHRIST. Amen.

DEVOTIONS FOR SPIRITUAL COMMUNION.

It happens sometimes that Christians, through distance of place, illness, or other unavoidable hindrances, are prevented from attending the Celebration of the Blessed Sacrament when they desire to do so. In this case it is proper that they should endeavour to be present in spirit, and unite themselves to those who are actually present at the Celebration.

It will be advisable that they should go to the place

where they generally say their prayers, and use such devotions as are applicable to the circumstances.

The following Form may be suitable: or so much of it as is possible.

Psalm xlii.
The Collect, Epistle, and Gospel for the day.
The Nicene Creed.
The Sanctus.

Then the following Prayer.

IN union, O dear LORD, with the faithful at every Altar of Thy Church, where Thy Death and Passion are pleaded before the FATHER, I desire to offer Thee praise and thanksgiving. I present unto Thee my soul and body, with the earnest wish that I may be ever united to Thee. And since I cannot now receive Thee sacramentally, I beseech Thee to come spiritually into my heart. I unite myself to Thee, and embrace Thee with all the affections of my soul. Oh, let nothing ever separate me from Thee ; let me live and die in Thy Love. Amen.

ANIMA CHRISTI.

SOUL of CHRIST, sanctify me ;
Body of CHRIST, save me ;
Blood of CHRIST, refresh me ;
Water from the Side of CHRIST, cleanse me ;
Passion of CHRIST, strengthen me ;
O good JESU, hear me ;
Within Thy Wounds hide me ;
Suffer me not to be separated from Thee ;
From the malicious enemy defend me ;
In the hour of my death call me ;
And bid me come to Thee,
That with Thy saints I may praise Thee,
For ever and ever. Amen.

Additional Devotions.

Devotions for Use in Sickness.

O LORD JESU CHRIST, I receive this sickness, with which Thou art pleased to visit me, as coming from Thy Fatherly hand. It is Thy Will, and therefore I submit ;—'not my will, but Thine be done.' May it be to the honour of Thy holy Name, and for the good of my soul ! I here offer myself with an entire submission to all Thine appointments; to suffer whatever Thou pleasest, as long as Thou pleasest, and in what manner Thou pleasest : for I am a creature, O LORD, who hast often and most ungratefully offended Thee, and whom Thou mightest justly have visited with Thy severest punishments. Oh, let Thy justice be tempered with mercy, and let Thy heavenly grace come to my assistance, to support me under this affliction ! Confirm my soul with strength from above, that I may bear with true Christian patience all the uneasiness, pains, disquiets, and troubles under which I labour; preserve me from all temptations and murmuring thoughts, that in this time of affliction I may in no way offend Thee ; and grant that this and all other earthly trials may be the means of preparing my soul for its passage into eternity, that, being purified from all my sins, I may believe in Thee, hope in Thee, love Thee above all things, and finally, through Thy infinite merits, be admitted into the company of the blessed in heaven, there to praise Thee for ever and ever. Amen.

O GOD, Who hast willed that we, who are appointed to death, should yet know neither the day nor the hour thereof ; grant to me Thy servant that I may walk before Thee in holiness and righteousness all my days, and finally depart in peace, and die in the LORD ; through JESUS CHRIST our LORD. Amen.

Ejaculatory Prayers for a Sick Person.

LORD, I accept this sickness from Thy hands, and entirely resign myself to Thy blessed will, whether it be for life or death.

2. Not my will, but Thine be done ; Thy Will be done on earth as it is in heaven.

3. LORD, I submit to all the pains and uneasiness of this my illness ; my sins have deserved infinitely more.

4. LORD, I offer up to Thee all that I now suffer, or may have yet to suffer, to be united to the Sufferings of my Redeemer, and sanctified by His Passion.

5. I worship Thee, O my GOD and my All, as my first Beginning and last End ; and I desire to bow down all the powers of my soul to Thee.

6. LORD, I desire to praise Thee constantly, in sickness as well as in health ; I desire to join my heart and voice with the whole Church of heaven and earth in blessing Thee for ever.

7. I give Thee thanks from the bottom of my heart for all Thy mercies and blessings bestowed upon me and Thy whole Church, through JESUS CHRIST Thy SON.

8. I thank Thee above all for having loved me from all eternity, and redeemed me with His precious Blood. Let not that Blood be shed for me in vain.

9. LORD, I believe all those heavenly truths which Thou hast revealed, and which Thy holy Catholic Church believes and teaches.

10. O my GOD, all my hope is in Thee ; and through the Passion and Death of JESUS CHRIST, my Redeemer, I hope for salvation from Thee. In Thee, O LORD, have I put my trust, let me never be put to confusion.

11. O sweet JESUS, receive me into Thine arms, in this day of my distress : hide me in Thy Wounds, bathe my soul in Thy precious Blood.

12. I love Thee, O my GOD, with my whole

heart and soul above all things ; at least I desire so to love Thee. Oh, come now, and take full possession of my whole soul, and teach me to love Thee for ever.

13. For Thy sake, O dear LORD, and because Thou hast loved me, I love my neighbour as myself; I forgive all who have injured or offended me, and I will endeavour to be reconciled to all whom I have injured or offended.

14. Have mercy upon me, O GOD, after Thy great goodness ; according to the multitude of Thy mercies do away mine offences.

15. Oh, that I had never offended so good a GOD ! Oh, that I had never sinned ! Happy those souls that have not lost their baptismal innocence !

16. I renounce from this moment, and for ever, the devil and all his works; and I abhor all his suggestions and temptations. Oh, suffer not, my LORD, this mortal enemy of my soul to have power over me, either now or at my last hour.

17. I commend my soul to GOD the FATHER Who created me ; to GOD the SON Who redeemed me with His precious Blood ; to GOD the HOLY GHOST Who sanctifieth me. Into Thy hands I commend my spirit, for Thou hast redeemed me, O LORD, Thou GOD of Truth.

In Pain.

O LORD JESU CHRIST, Who for the salvation of the world wast willing to bear with patience most grievous sorrows, Agony, Passion and Death ; make me, I beseech Thee, mindful of all that Thou hast borne for me ; give me strength to endure my afflictions for Thy sake, so that, sharing in Thy pain and sorrow, I may be made also a partaker of Thy rest and glory, who livest and reignest with the FATHER and the HOLY GHOST, one GOD, world without end. Amen.

O LORD JESU CHRIST, by Thy Cross and Passion strengthen me ; LORD, if Thou be willing, let this cup pass from me ; nevertheless not my will, but Thine be done.

When injured in Body.

O LORD, Who art the true Physician and Helper in sickness, and the Deliverer and Saviour from pain, heal me who have suffered grievous injury of body [restore me, if it be Thy will, to my former strength and power], have compassion upon me though I have in many things offended Thee, and deliver me, good JESU, from sin and from its punishment, that I may glorify Thy divine Power and bless Thy holy Name, Who livest and reignest with the FATHER and the HOLY GHOST, ever One GOD, world without end.   Amen.

For Patience.

O LORD JESU CHRIST, Who for my sake didst endure all manner of pains and distress of Body and Soul, grant me the grace of patience and resignation, that I may be enabled to endure what Thou art pleased to send me, as Thou wilt, and as long as Thou wilt, and grant that the weariness of my body may conduce to the good of my soul, who livest and reignest with the FATHER and the HOLY GHOST, ever One GOD, world without end.   Amen.

Before taking Medicine.

SEND Thy blessing, O LORD, upon the means I am now using for the recovery of my health, and grant that they may conduce to the relief of my sickness, and restore me if it be Thy good pleasure, through JESUS CHRIST our LORD.   Amen.

For a Happy Death.

O GOD OF MERCY, strengthen me with Thy heavenly grace, that at the hour of death the enemy may not prevail against me, but that I may be counted worthy to be carried by the Angels into the haven of rest.

Almighty and most merciful GOD, who broughtest out a fountain of water to refresh Thy thirsting people, bring forth from the hardness of my heart the tears of true repentance, that I may worthily bewail my sins, and be counted meet, by Thy mercy, to receive remission of all my sins, through JESUS CHRIST our LORD. Amen.

For Recovery.

O ALMIGHTY FATHER, in Whose hands are the issues of life and death, raise me up, I beseech Thee, if it be Thy will, from this bed of sickness; bless it to the good of my soul, and grant that I may spend all the years it shall please Thee to allow me here in holy obedience and true devotion to Thee, through JESUS CHRIST our LORD.

Thanksgiving for Relief or Recovery.

O GOD, Whose mercies are without number, and the treasure of Whose goodness is infinite, I give Thee hearty thanks for the blessings which Thou hast bestowed upon me, Thy unworthy servant, and I humbly beseech Thee that as Thou hast granted that for which I have prayed, so Thou wouldst continue Thy goodness towards me, and prepare me by Thy blessings in this life for the enjoyment of eternal happiness in the life to come; through JESUS CHRIST our LORD. Amen.

H

For the Fulfilment of Good Resolutions.

I YIELD Thee thanks, O LORD, for Thy mercies bestowed upon me in this time of sickness, and for the relief Thou hast of Thy gracious Goodness granted me ; I pray Thee that I may never forget Thy benefits, but may offer unto Thee the sacrifice of thanksgiving, and pay Thee my vows which I promised with my lips, and spake with my mouth when I was in trouble, through JESUS CHRIST our LORD. Amen.

Preparation for Death.

O MY GOD, I accept of death as a homage and adoration which I owe to Thy divine Majesty, and as a punishment justly due to my sins, in union with the Death of my dear Redeemer, and as the only means of coming to Thee, my first Beginning and last End.

I firmly believe all the sacred truths which the Catholic Church believeth and teacheth, because Thou hast revealed them. And by the assistance of Thy holy grace, I am resolved to live and die in the communion of this Thy Church.

Relying upon Thy goodness, power, and promises, I hope to obtain pardon of my sins, and life ever-lasting, through the merits of Thy SON JESUS CHRIST, my only Redeemer.

I love Thee with all my heart and soul, and desire to love Thee as the Blessed do in heaven. I adore all the designs of Thy divine Providence, resigning myself entirely to Thy Will.

I also love my neighbour for Thy sake, as I love myself. I sincerely forgive all who have injured me, and ask pardon of all whom I have injured.

I renounce the devil, with all his works ; the

world, with all its pomps; the flesh, with all its lusts.

I desire to be dissolved, and to be with CHRIST. FATHER, into Thy hands I commend my spirit. LORD JESUS, receive my soul.

May Almighty GOD have mercy on me and forgive me my sins, and bring me to life everlasting. Amen.

✠ May the Almighty and most merciful LORD grant me pardon, absolution, and remission of all my sins. Amen.

✠ GOD the FATHER, GOD the SON, and GOD the HOLY GHOST, have mercy upon me now and in the hour of death. Amen.

Acts of the Principal Virtues.

Prayer before the Acts.

ALMIGHTY and everlasting God, give unto us the increase of Faith, Hope, and Charity; and, that we may obtain that which Thou dost promise, make us to love that which Thou dost command; through JESUS CHRIST our LORD. Amen.

Act of Faith.

I MOST firmly believe, O my GOD, whatever Thy Holy Catholic Church believes and teaches, because Thou, Who art the unfailing Truth, hast revealed it. I believe that there is One GOD in Three Persons, the FATHER, the SON, and the HOLY GHOST. I believe that the Second Person, GOD the SON, became Man, suffered and died on the Cross for the redemption of the whole world; that He arose from the dead, ascended into heaven, and at the end of the world shall come to judge all mankind according to their works, rewarding the good with eternal

life in heaven, punishing the wicked in hell. In
this Faith I hope and resolve, O my GOD, by Thy
grace to live ; and in it, and if need be for it, to
die.

Act of Hope.

O MY GOD, relying on Thine almighty power,
and Thine infinite mercy and goodness, and
because Thou art faithful to Thy promises, I trust in
Thee that Thou wilt grant me forgiveness of my sins,
through the merits of JESUS CHRIST Thy SON ; and
that Thou wilt give me the assistance of Thy grace,
with which I may labour to continue to the end in
the diligent exercise of all good works, and may be
deemed worthy to obtain the glory which Thou hast
promised in heaven.

Act of Charity.

O LORD my GOD, I love Thee with my whole
heart, and above all things, because Thou, O
GOD, art the sovereign Good, and, for Thine own
infinite Perfections, art most worthy of all love ; and
for Thy sake I also love my neighbour as myself.

Act of Contrition.

O MY GOD, for the sake of Thy sovereign Goodness and infinite Perfection, which I love
above all things, I am exceedingly sorry for having
offended, by my sins, this Thine infinite Goodness ;
and I firmly resolve, by the assistance of Thy grace,
never more to offend Thee for the time to come, and
carefully to avoid the occasions of sin.

Act of Thanksgiving.

O MY GOD, I desire to give Thee thanks for all
Thine inestimable blessings and favours bestowed upon me. Thou hast thought of me, and

loved me from all eternity; Thou hast created me
for Thyself; Thou hast delivered up Thy beloved
SON to the shameful death of the Cross for my redemption; Thou hast made me a member of Thy
Holy Church; Thou hast preserved me from falling
into the abyss of eternal misery, when my sins had
provoked Thee to punish me; and Thou hast
graciously continued to spare me, even though I have
not ceased to offend Thee. What return, O my
GOD, can I make for Thy numberless blessings, and
the favours which Thou hast bestowed upon me?
May I unite with all Thy saints and angels in praising
and adoring Thee the GOD of all mercies, Who art so
bountiful to me Thy unworthy creature!

Penitential Prayers.

A Prayer suitable for Penitential Seasons.

O LORD JESU CHRIST, Very GOD and Very
Man, I grieve with my whole heart that I have
offended Thee, and I fully resolve by Thy help, and
for love of Thee, to shun all occasions of sin, and to
offend Thee no more.

O SAVIOUR of the world! Who gavest Thyself to
death and the Cross to save sinners, look on me, a
miserable sinner, who call upon Thy Name. If I
have done that for which Thou mayest condemn me,
Thou hast done that whereby Thou canst save me.
Spare me then, Thou that art my SAVIOUR, and pity
my sinful soul; loose its chains, heal its sores. I
desire Thee, LORD, I seek Thee, I yearn for Thee.
Show the light of Thy Countenance, and I shall be
whole.

May I live in Thee, die in Thee, and abide eternally in Thee. May I be wholly Thine, and Thou mine, O JESU, for ever, through Thy own merits. Amen.

I beseech Thee, O LORD, give a healing effect to this time of penitence, and sober living, that the mortification of our flesh may prove the nourishment of our souls: through JESUS CHRIST our LORD. Amen.

O merciful Redeemer! by all Thou hast done and suffered for poor sinners, grant to them all, I beseech Thee, the grace of conversion and true repentance, that they may return to Thee, the Shepherd and Bishop of their souls.

PRAYERS AGAINST THE SEVEN DEADLY SINS.[1]

Against Anger.

O MOST meek JESU, Prince of Peace, Who, when Thou wast reviled, reviledst not again, and on the Cross didst pray for Thy murderers; implant in our hearts the virtues of gentleness and patience, that we, restraining the fierceness of anger, impatience, and resentment, may overcome evil with good, for Thy sake may love our enemies, and as children of our heavenly FATHER seek Thy peace, and evermore rejoice in Thy love. Amen.

Against Pride.

O LORD JESU CHRIST, Pattern of humility, Who didst empty Thyself of Thy glory, and take upon Thee the form of a servant; root out of us all pride and swelling of heart, that owning ourselves

---

[1] These Prayers may be used in connection with the Seven Penitential Psalms, 6, 32, 38, 51, 102, 130, 143,

miserable and guilty sinners, we may willingly bear contempt and reproaches for Thy sake, and glorying in nothing save only in Thee, may esteem ourselves lowly in Thy sight. Not unto us, O LORD, not unto us, but to Thy Name be the praise, for Thy loving mercy, and for Thy truth's sake. Amen.

Against Gluttony.

O LORD JESU CHRIST, Mirror of abstinence, Who to teach us the virtue of abstinence didst fast forty days and forty nights; grant that serving Thee, and not our own appetites, we may live soberly and piously with contentment, without excess in food or in drink, that Thy Will being our nourishment, we may hunger and thirst after righteousness, and finally obtain from Thee that meat which endureth unto life eternal. Amen.

Against Lust.

O LORD JESU CHRIST, Guardian of chaste souls and Lover of purity, Who wast pleased to take our nature, and to be born of a pure Virgin; mercifully look upon my infirmity. Make me a clean heart, O GOD, and renew a right spirit within me; help me to drive away all evil thoughts, to conquer every sinful desire, and so pierce my flesh with the fear of Thee, that this bosom enemy being overcome, I may serve Thee with a chaste body and please Thee with a pure heart. Amen.

Against Covetousness.

O LORD JESU CHRIST, Who though Thou wast rich yet for our sakes didst become poor; grant that all over-eagerness and covetousness of earthly goods may die in us, and the desire of heavenly things may live and grow in us: keep us from

all idle and vain expenses, that we may have to give
to him that needeth, and that giving not grudgingly
nor of necessity, but cheerfully, we may be loved by
Thee, and be made through Thy merits partakers of
the riches of Thy heavenly treasure.

Against Envy.

O MOST loving JESU, Pattern of all charity,
Who makest all the commandments of the
law to consist in love towards GOD and towards man;
grant to us so to love Thee with all our heart, with
all our mind, and all our soul, and our neighbour
for Thy sake, that the grace of charity and brotherly
love may dwell in us, and all envy, harshness, and ill-
will may die in us; and fill our hearts with love,
kindness, and compassion, so that by constantly rejoicing in the happiness and good success of others,
by sympathising with them in their sorrows, and putting away all harsh judgments and envious thoughts,
we may follow Thee, Who art Thyself true and perfect
Charity.   Amen.

Against Sloth.

O LORD JESU CHRIST, Who in the Garden
didst pray so long and so fervently that Thy
sweat was as it were great drops of blood falling down
to the ground; put away from us, we beseech Thee,
all sloth and inactivity both of body and mind;
kindle within us the fire of Thy love, and strengthen
our weakness, that whatsoever our hand findeth to do
we may do it with all our might, and that striving
heartily to please Thee in this life, Thou mayest hereafter be our exceeding great reward,

PRAYERS FOR PARDON AND AMENDMENT.

O MOST sweet LORD JESU CHRIST, I, an unworthy sinner, would call to Thy memory all the holy thoughts which have been Thine from eternity until now; above all, that one by which Thou, O Eternal WORD, didst will to become man.

O most merciful LORD, I pray Thee, from the bottom of my heart, to pardon me all the vain, foul, and evil thoughts which, up to this hour, I have ever entertained, or in any way have caused others to entertain, against or beside Thy Will.

Our FATHER.

O MOST piteous LORD JESU CHRIST, I, a miserable sinner, would call to Thy memory all the good and saving words which Thou ever spakest when on earth.

I humbly pray Thee, O good JESU, to forgive me all the words which up to this hour I have uttered or caused others to utter, against Thy holy Will.

Our FATHER.

O MOST sweet JESU CHRIST, I, an unworthy sinner, yet redeemed by Thy precious Blood, would call to Thy memory all the good works which Thou wroughtest on the earth for our salvation.

I beseech Thee, most piteous LORD, pardon me whatsoever, by my ill deeds, I have at any time knowingly or ignorantly committed, or have caused others to commit, against Thy law, and the glory of Thy Name.

And now, O most gracious LORD, direct and order all my thoughts, words, and works, according to Thy good pleasure, and to the praise of Thy

Name; and conform them to the perfect pattern of Thy most holy Life and Conversation. Thine I am, and will be, O LORD, in life and in death; into Thy hands I commend myself, and all that I am and have.

Our FATHER.

Devotions on the Passion.

O LORD JESU CHRIST, Who hast said, No man can come to Me except he deny himself, and take up his cross, and follow Me; grant, we beseech Thee, that venerating Thy blessed Patience in bearing Thy Cross, and being borne upon it, I may bear all the crosses and trials of this valley of tears; that being purified by suffering, I may be admitted into Thy eternal rest, Who livest and reignest with the FATHER and the HOLY GHOST, ever One GOD, world without end.

O JESU CHRIST, my only SAVIOUR, Thy Death and most bitter Passion was for me; let it not be without its fruit, and useless to me, a miserable sinner. By all Thy shame, by Thy most agonising Death and wounded Heart, give me Thy grace, now and in the hour of death. Amen.

O GOOD Shepherd, CHRIST JESU, Who dost cleanse and feed Thy sheep with Thine own precious Blood; may the plenteous outpouring of Thy most holy Blood be to me and to all poor sinners comfort and salvation. Amen.

O JESU of Nazareth, King of the Jews, by the victory and the triumph won on the Cross against Thy enemies and ours, save me from mine. Guard from all peril my soul and body. Give Thy Church concord and peace; to the departed, rest and peace; to sinners, repentance and forgiveness; grace and mercy to all. Amen.

O JESU, our High Priest, Who offeredst to GOD the FATHER a pure Oblation, mighty to reconcile sinners unto GOD; by the infinite merits of Thy Life, Thy Passion, and Death, make me die to the world, and live to Thee alone: and then let Thy servant depart in peace. Amen.

I WILL lay me down at the foot of the Cross and know no rest save in Thee, O my LORD and SAVIOUR.

Prayer before the Cross.

MOST gracious and loving JESU, I come to Thee for refuge. I return to Thee all-loving; but, O LORD, when I look on these Thy Wounds, and see Thy Crown of thorns, and remember that for my sake Thou didst suffer all these things, I am covered with shame and confusion. For it is I, even I, who smote Thee with these cruel Wounds; it is I who pressed these thorns into Thy sacred Temples; even I who nailed Thee to the Cross. Thy Love, Thy Mercy, Thy Pity,—Oh, who shall tell? It was I who sinned; and yet for me Thou didst endure the punishment. Thou hast paid the penalty of death for me. I was Thy enemy: by Thy Cross Thou makest me a son. I was a slave; but by Thy Blood Thou hast made me free. O that Thou wouldst kindle the flame of Thy love within me, that I might wholly burn with love for Thee; then will I, who owe Thee myself and all I have, gladly spend my very life for Thee. Amen.

Another Prayer.

O LORD JESU CHRIST, Son of the Living God, interpose Thy Passion, Cross, and Death between Thy Judgment and my soul, now and in the hour of my death.

Vouchsafe to give me grace and mercy, pardon to all sinners, peace to Thy Church, and the consummation of happiness to all Thine elect; Who livest and reignest with the FATHER and the HOLY SPIRIT, ever one GOD, world without end.   Amen.

O JESU CHRIST, my only Redeemer, suffer not the fruits of Thy Passion to be lost on me.

O Good Shepherd, Who with Thy Blood feedest and healest Thy sheep, grant that the shedding thereof may cleanse my soul from all sin.

O Divine SON, obedient to the FATHER, Who didst willingly drink the bitter cup of Thy Passion, grant that through Thy grace I may be obedient to the FATHER, even unto death.

O Eternal FATHER, look on the Face of Thy CHRIST, and accept the Sacrifice He offers Thee on the Cross.   May His Sufferings and Death be a propitiation for my sins !

O by Thine unknown sufferings,
    Good LORD, deliver me.

Our FATHER.

O SAVIOUR of the world, Who by Thy Cross and Precious Blood hast redeemed us, save us and help us, we humbly beseech Thee, O LORD.   Amen.

COLLECTS,

WHICH MAY BE USED AT EACH OF THE SEVEN CANONICAL HOURS.

Matins.

O LORD JESU, by the Love wherewith Thou didst love Thine own, even unto the end, by the bloody Sweat which fell down from Thee in the Garden ; by the spite and griefs which Thou didst endure when Thy disciple sold Thee, and the wicked Jews bound and rent Thee ; unbind the chains of my sins, and bind this my soul with the most strait bonds of love, which cannot be unloosed ; Who livest, &c.

Prime. (6 A.M.)

O LORD JESU, Who at the hour of *Prime* wast brought before Pontius Pilate, the Heavenly before an earthly Judge, and by the wicked priests wast falsely charged with evil deeds ; help us miserable sinners in the Judgment Day, that we be not doomed with wicked men to endless punishment, but be made worthy of the fellowship of Thy saints in heavenly places ; Who livest, &c.

Terce. (9 A.M.)

O LORD JESU, Who at the *third hour* of the day wast beaten with scourges, and crowned with thorns, grant that we, Thy servants, having our bodies subdued by voluntary chastisement, may be deemed worthy members of Thee, our thorn-crowned Head ; Who livest, &c.

Sext. (12 A.M.)

O LORD JESU, Who at the *sixth hour* didst hang with pierced Feet and Hands from the wood of the Cross, and didst fasten thereto with the same nails the handwriting of our condemnation; grant to my soul that, thus set free from the service of sin, I may ever bear in my heart of hearts as the symbols of my deliverance, those Thy most Holy Wounds ; Who livest, &c.

None. (3 P.M.)

O LORD JESU, Who at the *ninth hour*, when all was finished, didst bow Thy Head, and yield Thy Spirit to Thy FATHER, and breathe into mankind, who lay in death, the breath of life ; grant that I, who do owe myself wholly to Thee for making me, may, now that Thou hast remade me, yield Thee myself wholly again, and live henceforth no more unto myself, but always unto Thee, Who didst vouchsafe to die for me, and Who livest, &c.

Vespers. (6 P.M.)

O LORD JESU, Who at the *evening hour* didst will that Thy lifeless Body should be taken from the Cross and be laid in Thy most holy Mother's arms ; grant me never, while I live, to put from me my Cross, which in Thy Goodness Thou mayst bestow on me ; and when I die and am taken from it, make me worthy to be presented before Thee, and be received in the arms of Thy Mercy; Who livest, &c.

Compline. (9 P.M.)

O LORD JESU, Who at the hour of *Compline* didst rest in the grave, and wast mourned by Thy sad Mother and the other women, give us true tears to weep for Thy most holy Passion, and grant us never to do that which may crucify Thee afresh ; Who livest, &c.

Devotions for Communion.

AN EXERCISE BEFORE HOLY COMMUNION.[1]

1. *Direction of the Intention.*

LORD JESU, King of everlasting glory, behold I desire to come to Thee [this day] and to receive Thy Body and Blood in this heavenly Sacrament, for Thy honour and glory, and the good of my soul. I desire to receive Thee, because it is Thy desire, and Thou hast so ordained : blessed be Thy Name for ever. I desire to come to Thee like the Magdalene, that I may be delivered from all my evils and embrace Thee, my only Good. I desire to come to Thee that I may be happily united to Thee, that I may henceforth abide in Thee, and Thou in me ; and that nothing in life or death may ever separate me from Thee. I desire to come to Thee, humbly beseeching Thee to grant me (*here name your special intention*), by the infinite merits of the Sacrifice of Thy Life, Passion, and Death.

2. *Act of Humility.*

O MY GOD, how shall I dare to approach unto Thee—so wretched a worm to so infinite a Majesty—so unclean a sinner to such infinite Purity and Holiness? My soul is wholly covered with leprosy, and how shall I presume to embrace Thee? I tremble at the sentence of Thine Apostle, that he that receiveth unworthily receiveth his own condemnation ; for I cannot but acknowledge myself infinitely unworthy ; nor should I dare ever to come to Thee, were I not called by Thy most loving invitation, and encouraged by Thine infinite Goodness

---

[1] This Exercise may, if preferred, be divided to correspond with the days of the week, or otherwise.

and Mercy.   In this Mercy, which is above all Thy
works, I put my whole trust ; and in this confidence
alone I presume to draw nigh unto Thee.

3. *Act of Faith.*

I MOST firmly believe, O JESU, that in this holy
Sacrament Thou art present verily and indeed ;
that here is Thy Body and Blood, Thy Soul and Thy
Divinity.   I believe that Thou, my SAVIOUR, true
GOD and true Man, art really here, with all Thy
treasures ; that here Thou communicatest Thyself to
us, makest us partakers of the fruit of Thy Passion, and
givest us a Pledge of eternal life. I believe there cannot
be a greater happiness than to receive Thee worthily,
nor a greater misery than to receive Thee unworthily.
All this I most steadfastly believe, because it is what
Thou hast taught us in Thy Word, and by Thy
Church. .

4. *Act of Contrition.*

O LORD, I detest, with my whole heart, all the
sins by which I have offended Thy divine
Majesty, from the first moment that I was capable
of sinning to this very hour.   I desire to lay them all
at Thy Feet, to be cancelled by Thy precious Blood.
Hear me, O LORD, by that infinite Love by which Thou
hast shed Thy Blood for me.   Oh, let not that Blood
be shed in vain for me ! I detest my sins, because
they have offended Thy infinite Goodness.   By Thy
grace I will never commit them any more : I am
sorry for them, and will be sorry for them as long as
I live ; and according to the best of my power, will
do penance for them.   Forgive me, dear LORD, for
Thy mercy's sake ; pardon me all that is past ; and
be Thou my Keeper for the time to come, that I may
never more offend Thee.

5. *Act of Love.*

O LORD JESU, the GOD of my heart, and the Life of my soul, as the hart pants after the water-brooks, so doth my soul pant after Thee, the Fountain of life and the Ocean of all good. I rejoice that I am to go into the house of the LORD; or rather that my LORD is to come into my house and take up His abode with me. O happy moment, when I shall be admitted to the Presence of the living God, Whom my soul desires to receive! Come, LORD JESU, and take full possession of my heart for ever! I offer it to Thee without reserve; I desire to consecrate it eternally to Thee. I love Thee with my whole soul above all things; at least, I desire so to love Thee. It is nothing less than infinite Love that brings Thee to me; O teach me to make a due return to Thee!

6. *Commemoration of the Passion of Christ.*

I DESIRE, in these Holy Mysteries, to commemorate, as Thou hast commanded, all Thy Sufferings; Thy Agony and Bloody Sweat; Thy being betrayed and apprehended; all the reproaches and calumnies, all the scoffs and affronts, all the blows and buffets, Thou hast endured for me; Thy being scourged, crowned with thorns, and loaded with a heavy cross for my sins, and for those of the whole world; Thy Crucifixion and Death, together with Thy glorious Resurrection and triumphant Ascension. I adore Thee, and give Thee thanks for all that thou hast done and suffered for us; and for giving us, in the most Blessed Sacrament, this Pledge of our Redemption, this Victim of our ransom, this Body and Blood which was offered for us.

I

7. *Prayer for Grace.*

O MY GOD, thou knowest my great poverty and misery, and that of myself I can do nothing ; Thou knowest how unworthy I am of this infinite favour, and Thou alone canst make me worthy. Since Thou art so good to call me thus to Thyself, add this one bounty more to all the rest, to prepare me for Thyself. Cleanse my soul from its stains, clothe it with the wedding garment of charity, adorn it with all virtues, and make it a fit abode for Thee. Drive sin and the devil far from this dwelling, which Thou art here pleased to choose for Thyself, and make me one according to Thy own heart ; that this heavenly visit, which Thou designest for my salvation, may not, by my unworthiness, be perverted to my own condemnation. Let me never be guilty of Thy Body and Blood by an unworthy communion. For the sake of this same Precious Blood, which Thou hast shed for me, deliver me, O JESU, from so great an evil.

ACTS OF DEVOTION, PRAISE, AND THANKS-GIVING AFTER COMMUNION.

O LORD JESU CHRIST, my Creator and my Redeemer, my GOD and my All, whence is this to me, that my LORD, and so great a LORD, whom heaven and earth cannot contain, should come into this poor dwelling, this house of clay of my earthly habitation ? Bow down thyself, with all thy powers, O my soul, to adore the sovereign Majesty which hath vouchsafed to come to visit thee ; pay Him the best homage thou art able, as to thy first Beginning, and thy last End ; pour thyself forth in His presence in praise and thanksgiving ; and invite all heaven and earth to join with thee in magnifying their LORD and thine, for His mercy and bounty to thee.

What return shall I make to Thee, O LORD, for all Thou hast done for me? Behold, when I had no being at all, Thou didst create me; and when I was gone astray, and lost in my sins, Thou didst redeem me by dying for me. All that I have, all that I am, is Thy gift; and now, after all Thy other favours, Thou hast given me Thyself: blessed be Thy Name for ever! Thou art great, O LORD, and exceedingly to be praised; great are Thy works, and of Thy Wisdom there is no end; but Thy tender mercies, Thy Bounty and Goodness to me, are above all Thy works; these I desire to confess and extol for ever.

Bless, then, thy LORD, O my soul, and let all that is within thee praise and magnify His holy Name. Bless the LORD, O my soul, and see thou never forget all that He hath done for thee. O all ye works of the LORD, bless ye the LORD, praise Him and magnify Him for ever. O all ye angels of the LORD, bless ye the LORD, praise Him and magnify Him for ever. Bless the LORD all ye saints, and let the whole Church of heaven and earth join in praising and giving Him thanks for all His mercies and graces to me; and so, in some measure, supply what is due from me. But, O LORD, as all this still falls short of what I owe Thee for Thy infinite Love, I offer to Thee, O Eternal FATHER, the same SON of Thine Whom Thou hast given me, and His Thanksgiving, which is infinite in value. Look not, then, upon my insensibility and ingratitude, but upon the Face of Thy Christ, and with Him, and through Him, receive this offering of my poor self, which I desire to make to Thee.

ASPIRATIONS AFTER COMMUNION.

WHO art Thou, O LORD, and what am I? Dost Thou come unto me, O King most High, even to the very lowest of Thy servants?

Behold, O LORD, I now have Thee, Who hast all things : I possess Thee, Who possessest all things, and canst do all things ; therefore, O my GOD and my All, do Thou wean my heart from all other things beside Thee, for in them there is nothing but vanity and vexation of spirit ; on Thee alone may my heart be fixed ; in Thee be my rest, for in Thee is my treasure, in Thee is the sovereign truth, and true happiness and eternal life.

Let my soul, O LORD, feel the sweetness of Thy presence. May it taste how sweet Thou art, O LORD, that, allured by love of Thee, it may seek for nothing wherein to rejoice out of Thee ; for Thou art the Joy of my heart, and my GOD, and my Portion for ever.

Thou art the Physician of my soul, Who with Thine own stripes hast healed our sickness. I am that sick soul whom Thou camest from Heaven to heal ; heal my soul therefore, for I have sinned against Thee.

Thou art the Good Shepherd Who hast laid down Thy life for Thy sheep. Behold, I am that sheep which was lost, and yet Thou dost vouchsafe to heal me with Thy Body and Blood ; lay me now upon Thy shoulders. What wilt Thou refuse me Who hast given Thyself unto me ? Oh, be Thou my Shepherd, and I shall lack nothing in the green pasture wherein Thou feedest me, until I am brought to the pastures of eternal life.

O Thou true Light, which enlightenest every man that cometh into the world, enlighten my eyes, that I sleep not in death.

O Fire continually burning and never failing ! Behold how lukewarm and cold I am ; Oh, do Thou inflame my reins and my heart that they may be on fire with the love of Thee. For Thou camest to send fire on the earth, and what wilt Thou but that it be kindled ?

O King of heaven and earth, rich in pity! Behold I am poor and needy; Thou knowest what I most require; Thou alone art able to enrich and help me; help me, O GOD, and out of the treasure of Thy Goodness succour Thou my needy soul.

O my LORD and my GOD! Behold I am Thy servant; give me understanding, and kindle my affections that I may know and do Thy will.

Thou art the Lamb of GOD, the Lamb without spot, Who takest away the sins of the world; take away from me whatever hurteth me and displeaseth Thee; and give me what Thou knowest to be pleasing to Thee and good for me.

Thou art my Love and all my Joy; Thou art the Portion of mine inheritance and of my cup; Thou art He Who shall maintain my lot.

O my GOD and my All! may the sweet and burning power of Thy Love, I beseech Thee, absorb my soul, that I may die unto the world for the love of Thee, Who for the love of me hast vouchsafed to die upon the Cross, O my GOD and my All!

PETITIONS TO JESUS SUFFERING.

For use during the Celebration.

O CHRIST JESU, meek and humble of heart, Who, being in the form of GOD, didst empty Thyself, and take upon Thee the form of a servant; grant that my heart may not be lifted up, that I be not high-minded, but fear.

O MY GOD, Who, when Thou wast rich, didst take upon Thee the form of a poor Servant, incline my heart to Thy testimonies, that I may delight in the way of Thy commandments.

O Lamb without spot, Who didst will to be born of a Virgin; grant me purity of mind and body, by

that wine which maketh virgins. Create in me a
clean heart, O God !

O CHRIST JESU, who wast led as an innocent
Lamb to the slaughter, and didst suffer so many
injuries and reproaches ; grant me the spirit of
patience and meekness. May I learn of Thee to be
meek and humble of heart !

O CHRIST my SAVIOUR, Who when Thou didst
thirst wast given gall and vinegar to drink, but hast
prepared for us all spiritual joys in this Sacrament ;
detach me from all sensual gratifications. Grant
that I may serve Thee, my GOD, not the flesh ; take
away from me all sensual lusts, that my heart may
never be defiled by sin.

O LORD, Who in the garden didst pray long and
fervently with a bloody Sweat ; grant that I may
praise Thee with my whole heart, and enjoy the
comfort of Thy holy grace.

O LORD, Who with true charity didst pray for
Thine enemies ; grant me to love my neighbour as
myself, and to bless them that hate me.

O most sweet SAVIOUR and Searcher of hearts,
Thou knowest what is in man, Thou spiest out all
my ways, Thou knowest better than I do the virtues
and gifts which I need most in the station of life
wherein Thy providence has placed me. Grant me
then Thy grace, O Thou Who hast given me so plenteous a Treasure, even Thyself, the Author of grace, in
this Sacrament ! For what good shall be wanting to
him to whom the very Author of good deigns to
come as a Guest ? When Thou, O LORD, didst
enter into the house of Zacchæus, Thou saidst,
' This day is Salvation come to this house.' Say to
my soul, I beseech Thee, O LORD, ' I am thy
Salvation.'

Hymns.

I.

Act of Contrition.

GOD of mercy and compassion,
    Look with pity upon me ;
FATHER ! let me call Thee Father !
'Tis Thy child returns to Thee !
    JESU ! LORD ! I ask for mercy,
    Let me not implore in vain !
    All my sins—I now detest them
    Never would I sin again.

By my sins I have deserved
    Death and endless misery ;
Hell, with all its pains and torments,
    And for all eternity.
                  JESU ! LORD ! &c.

By my sins I have abandoned
    Right and claim to Heaven above ;
Where the saints rejoice for ever
    In a boundless sea of love.
                  JESU ! LORD ! &c.

See our SAVIOUR, bleeding, dying,
    On the Cross of Calvary ;
To that Cross my sins have nailed Him,
    Yet He bleeds and dies for me.
                  JESU ! LORD ! &c.

II.

τὰς ἑδρὰς τὰς αἰωνίας.

THOSE eternal bowers
    Man hath never trod,
Those unfading flowers
    Round the throne of GOD.

Who may hope to gain them
  After weary fight?
Who at length attain them
  Clad in robes of white?

He, who gladly barters
  All on earthly ground;
He who, like the martyrs,
  Says ' I will be crowned ' :
He, whose one oblation
  Is a life of love;
Clinging to the nation
  Of the blest above.

Shame upon you, legions
  Of the Heavenly King,
Denizens of regions
  Past imagining!
What! with pipe and tabor
  Fool away the light,
When He bids you labour, —
  When He tells you—' Fight.'

While I do my duty,
  Struggling through the tide,
Whisper Thou of beauty
  On the other side!
Tell who will the story
  Of this life's distress;
Oh, the future glory!
  Oh, the loveliness!

III.

THE King of love my Shepherd is,
    Whose Goodness faileth never;
I nothing lack if I am His
  And He is mine for ever.

Where streams of living water flow
  My ransomed soul He leadeth,
And, where the verdant pastures grow,
  With food celestial feedeth.

Perverse and foolish oft I strayed,
  But yet in love He sought me,
And on His shoulder gently laid,
  And home, rejoicing, brought me.

In death's dark vale I fear no ill
  With Thee, dear LORD, beside me ;
Thy rod and staff my comfort still,
  Thy Cross before to guide me.

Thou spread'st a Table in my sight ;
  Thy Unction grace bestoweth ;
And oh, what transport of delight
  From Thy pure Chalice floweth !

And so through all the length of days
  Thy Goodness faileth never ;
Good Shepherd, may I sing Thy praise
  Within Thy house for ever.

[By permission of the Editors of 'Hymns Ancient and
Modern.']

IV.

Veni Creator Spiritus.

COME, HOLY GHOST, our souls inspire,
  And lighten with celestial fire.

Thou the anointing Spirit art,
Who dost Thy sevenfold gifts impart.

Thy blessèd Unction from above
Is comfort, life, and fire of love.

Enable with perpetual light
The dulness of our blinded sight.

Anoint and cheer our soilèd face
With the abundance of Thy grace.

Keep far our foes, give peace at home :
Where Thou art guide, no ill can come.

Teach us to know the FATHER, SON,
And Thee of both to be but One,

That, through the ages all along,
This may be our endless song ;

Praise to Thy eternal merit,
FATHER, SON, and HOLY SPIRIT. Amen.

V.

The Seven Gifts of the Holy Spirit.

SPIRIT of WISDOM ! guide Thine own,
Who make Thee now their choice ;
That they may never walk alone,
But hear Thy heavenly voice.

SPIRIT of UNDERSTANDING ! Light
That this world never saw ;
Open their eyes to see aright
The wonders of Thy law.

SPIRIT of COUNSEL ! 'neath the cloud
Of sorrow and dismay,
Cheer Thou their souls with grief when bowed,
And chase all doubt away.

SPIRIT of STRENGTH ! infuse Thy might,
Nerve Thy young soldiers' arms ;
Temptation let them put to flight,
And banish Hell's alarms.

SPIRIT of KNOWLEDGE ! Whose deep things,
  Are now but darkly shown,
Lead them on Resurrection wings
  To know as they are known.

SPIRIT of GODLINESS ! unfold
  The joys of heavenly grace,
Give peace on earth,—the bliss untold
  Of saints who see Thy face.

SPIRIT of Holy FEAR ! inspire
  Dread reverence of Thy Name,
That we with the celestial choir
  May praise Thee without blame.

Hear us, O HOLY TRINITY,
  Whom Heaven and earth adore,
To Whom be laud and honour done
  Both now and evermore.

VI.

PRAISE to the Holiest in the height,
    And in the depth be praise ;
In all His words most wonderful,
  Most sure in all His ways !

O loving wisdom of our GOD,
  When all was sin and shame,
A second Adam to the fight
  And to the rescue came.

O wisest love ! that flesh and blood
  Which did in Adam fail,
Should strive afresh against their foe,
  Should strive, and should prevail ;

And that a higher gift than grace
  Should flesh and blood refine,
GOD'S Presence and His very Self
  And Essence all-divine.

O generous love ! that He Who smote
  In man for man the foe,
The double agony in man
  For man should undergo ;

And in the garden secretly,
  And on the Cross on high,
Should teach His brethren and inspire
  To suffer and to die.

Praise to the Holiest in the height,
  And in the depth be praise :
In all His words most wonderful,
  Most sure in all His ways !

VII.

Before a Celebration.

IN the Name of GOD the FATHER,
  In the Name of GOD the SON,
In the Name of GOD the SPIRIT,
  One in Three, and Three in One ;
In the Name which highest Angels
  Speak not ere they veil their face,
Crying, ' Holy, Holy, Holy,'
  Come we to this sacred place.

Lo, in wondrous condescension,
  JESUS seeks His Altar-throne,
Though in lowly symbols hidden,
  Faith and love His Presence own.
When the LORD His Temple visits,
  Let the listening earth be still,
May the SPIRIT's sweet indwelling
  Each believing heart fulfil.

Here in figure represented
  See the Passion once again ;
Here behold the Lamb most Holy
  As for our redemption slain ;
Here the SAVIOUR'S Body broken,
  Here the Blood which JESUS shed,
Mystic Food of Life eternal
  See for our refreshment spread.

Here shall highest praise be offered,
  Here shall meekest prayer be poured,
Here, with body, soul, and spirit,
  GOD Incarnate be adored.
Holy JESU, for Thy coming
  May Thy love our hearts prepare ;
Thine we fain would have been wholly,
  Enter, LORD, and tarry there.

VIII.

Tantum ergo.

THUS in thankful love adoring
  We His unseen Presence hail ;
Older forms their place resigning,
  Newer Rites of grace prevail ;
Willing faith all want supplying
  Where our feebler senses fail.

Praise to GOD, the Eternal FATHER,
  Praise to GOD, the Eternal SON,
Praise to GOD, the Eternal SPIRIT,
  ONE in THREE, and THREE in ONE.
Honour, praise, salvation, blessing,
  Now and evermore be done.

IX.

O salutaris Hostia.

O SAVING VICTIM, opening wide
   The gate of heaven to man below,
Our foes press on from every side ;
   Thine aid supply ; Thy strength bestow.

To GOD, the THREE in ONE, ascend
   All thanks and praise for evermore ;
O grant us life that shall not end
   Upon the heavenly country's shore.

X.

ONCE, only once, and once for all,
   His precious life He gave :
Before the Cross our spirits fall
   And own it strong to save.

'One offering single and complete,'
   With lips and heart we say ;
But what He never can repeat
   He shows forth day by day.

For, as the priest of Aaron's line
   Within the Holiest stood,
And sprinkled o'er the mercy shrine
   With sacrificial Blood ;

So He, Who once atonement wrought,
   Our Priest of endless power,
Presents Himself for those He bought
   In that dark noontide hour.

His Manhood pleads where now It lives
　　On Heaven's eternal Throne,
And where in mystic Rite He gives
　　Its Presence to His Own.

And so we show Thy Death, O LORD,
　　Till Thou again appear,
And feel, when we approach Thy Board,
　　We have an Altar here.

All glory to the FATHER be,
　　All glory to the SON,
All glory, HOLY GHOST, to Thee,
　　While endless ages run.

XI.

AND now, O Father, mindful of the Love
　　That bought us, once for all, on Calvary's Tree,
And having with us Him that pleads above,
　　We here present, we here spread forth to Thee
That only Offering perfect in Thine eyes,
　　The one, true, pure, immortal Sacrifice.

Look, Father, look on His Anointed Face,
　　And only look on us as found in Him;
Look not on our misusings of Thy grace,
　　Our prayer so languid, and our faith so dim;
For lo! between our sins and their reward
　　We set the Passion of Thy Son our Lord.

And then for those, our dearest and our best,
　　By this prevailing Presence we appeal;
Oh, fold them closer to Thy Mercy's breast,
　　Oh, do Thine utmost for their souls' true weal;
From tainting mischief keep them white and clear
　　And crown Thy gifts with strength to persevere.

And so we come ; Oh, draw us to Thy feet,
  Most patient Saviour, Who canst love us still,
And by this Food, so awful and so sweet,
  Deliver us from every touch of ill ;
In Thine own service make us glad and free
  And grant us never more to fall from Thee.

XII.

WE pray Thee, heavenly FATHER,
    To hear us in Thy love,
And pour upon Thy children
  The unction from above ;
That so in love abiding,
  From all defilement free,
We may in pureness offer
  Our Eucharist to Thee.

Be Thou our Guide and Helper,
  O JESU CHRIST, we pray ;
So may we well approach Thee,
  If Thou wilt be the Way :
Thou, very Truth, hast promised
  To help us in our strife,
Food of the weary pilgrim,
  Eternal Source of Life.

And Thou, Creator SPIRIT,
  Look on us—we are Thine ;
Renew in us Thy graces,
  Upon our darkness shine ;
That with Thy benediction
  Upon our souls outpoured,
We may receive in gladness
  The Body of the LORD.

O TRINITY of Persons,
  O UNITY most High !
On Thee alone relying
  Thy servants would draw nigh :

Unworthy in our weakness,
On Thee our hope is stayed,
And blest by Thy forgiveness
We will not be afraid.

XIII.

ALLELUIA ! sing to JESUS !
His the sceptre, His the throne ;
Alleluia ! His the triumph,
His the victory alone ;
Hark ! the songs of peaceful Sion
Thunder like a mighty flood,
JESUS out of every nation
Hath redeemed us by His Blood.

Alleluia ! not as orphans
We are left in sorrow now ;
Alleluia ! He is near us,
Faith believes, nor questions how ;
Though the cloud from sight received Him
When the forty days were o'er,
Shall our hearts forget His promise—
' I am with you evermore ' ?

Alleluia ! Bread of Angels,
Thou on earth our Food, our Stay ;
Alleluia ! here the sinful
Flee to Thee from day to day ;
Intercessor, Friend of sinners,
Earth's REDEEMER, plead for me,
Where the songs of all the sinless
Sweep across the crystal sea.

Alleluia ! King Eternal,
Thee the LORD of lords we own ;
Alleluia ! born of Mary,
Earth Thy footstool, Heaven Thy throne.

K

Thou within the veil hast entered,
  Robed in flesh, our great High Priest ;
Thou on earth both Priest and Victim
  In the Eucharistic Feast.

Alleluia ! sing to JESUS !
  His the sceptre, His the throne ;
Alleluia ! His the triumph,
  His the victory alone ;
Hark ! the songs of peaceful Sion
  Thunder like a mighty flood ;
JESUS out of every nation
  Hath redeemed us by His Blood.

XIV.

O JESU LORD, remember
    When Thou shalt come again
Upon the clouds of Heaven,
  With all Thy shining train ;

When every eye shall see Thee
  In Deity revealed,
Who here upon this Altar
  In silence art concealed ;—

Remember, then, O SAVIOUR,
  I supplicate of Thee,
That here I bowed before Thee
  Upon my bended knee ;

That here I owned Thy Presence,
  And did not Thee deny ;
And glorified Thy greatness,
  Though hid from human eye.

Accept, Divine Redeemer,
  The homage of my praise,
Be Thou the Light and Honour,
  And Glory of my days.

Be Thou my Consolation
  When death is drawing nigh ;
Be Thou my only Treasure
  Through all eternity.   Amen.

XV.

Thanksgiving after Communion.

JESU, gentlest SAVIOUR,
  GOD of might and power ;
Thou Thyself art dwelling
  In us at this hour.

Nature cannot hold Thee,
  Heaven is all too strait
For Thine endless glory
  And Thy royal state.

Out beyond the shining
  Of the farthest star,
Thou art ever stretching
  Infinitely far.

Yet the hearts of children
  Hold what worlds cannot ;
And the GOD of wonders
  Loves the lowly spot.

JESU, gentlest SAVIOUR !
  Thou art in us now ;
Fill us with Thy Goodness,
  Till our hearts o'erflow.

Pray the prayer within us
  That to Heaven shall rise ;
Sing the song that angels
  Sing above the skies.
                K 2

Multiply our graces,
　　Chiefly love and fear,
And, dear LORD, the chiefest,
　　Grace to persevere.

Oh, how can we thank Thee
　　For a Gift like this—
Gift that truly maketh
　　Heaven's eternal bliss.

Ah ! when wilt Thou always
　　Make our hearts Thy home
We must wait for Heaven,
　　Then the day shall come.

XVI.

The Seven Words on the Cross.

JESU hail !   Who, as Thou bleedest
　　For Thy cruel murderers pleadest,
　　' Father, spare, their sins forgive ; '
Give us hearts like Thine forgiving,
Tenderest words like Thine conceiving,
　　Let no thought of vengeance live.

JESU hail ! in death Who savest,
Who the contrite robber gavest
　　Earnest of Thy blissful Face.
Grant our tears such pleading power
Now and at our dying hour,
　　As may win Thy pardoning grace.

JESU hail ! Thy Mother weeping
To Thy loved disciple's keeping
　　From Thy Cross Who dost commend ;
With like tender care assure us,
With like constant care secure us,
　　In all straits our lasting Friend.

JESU hail ! with death-cry shaken,
' FATHER, why hast Thou forsaken ? '
   In Thy last strong Agony.
Ne'er from us Thy presence sever,
May we stand beside Thee ever,
   In our troubles be Thou nigh.

JESU hail ! Whose word ' I thirst '
Mock Thy foes with draught accurst,
   Thou, Who dost all needs supply.
Make us thirst for heavenly treasures,
Earth's low joys and fleeting pleasures
   Passing with untempted eye.

JESU hail ! Thou hast completed
All Thy FATHER's Will ; and meted
   Unto us Thy merits blest.
LORD, to Thee our first thoughts bending,
And in Thee our last works ending
   In Thy pleasure let us rest.

JESU hail ! Thy words who closest,
And Thy outpoured Soul reposest
   Meekly in Thy FATHER's breast ;
Let Thy death with cleansing power
O'er our lives Thy graces shower ;
   Be our deaths by Thee most blest !

Litanies.

LITANY OF THE HOLY NAME OF JESUS.

LORD, have mercy upon us :
  CHRIST, have mercy upon us.
Lord, have mercy upon us.
Jesus, hear us :
JESUS, graciously hear us.
O GOD the FATHER, of Heaven,
O GOD the SON, Redeemer of the world,
O GOD the HOLY GHOST,
O HOLY TRINITY, one GOD,
JESUS, SON of the living GOD,
JESUS, Splendour of the FATHER,
JESUS, Brightness of Eternal Light,
JESUS, King of Glory,
JESUS, Sun of Righteousness,
JESUS, Son of the Virgin Mary,
JESUS, most wonderful,
JESUS, the mighty GOD,
JESUS, the everlasting FATHER,
JESUS, the Angel of great counsel,
JESUS, most powerful,
JESUS, most patient,
JESUS, most obedient,
JESUS, meek and humble of Heart,
JESUS, Lover of chastity,
JESUS, Lover of men,
JESUS, God of peace,
JESUS, Author of life,
JESUS, Example of virtues,
JESUS, zealous Lover of souls,
JESUS, our GOD,
JESUS, our Refuge,
JESUS, Father of the poor,
JESUS, Treasure of the faithful,

Have mercy upon us.

Jesus, Good Shepherd,
Jesus, true Light,
Jesus, eternal Wisdom,
Jesus, infinite Goodness,
Jesus, the Way, the Truth, and the Life,
Jesus, joy of Angels,
Jesus, King of Patriarchs,
Jesus, Master of Apostles,
Jesus, Teacher of Evangelists,
Jesus, Strength of Martyrs,
Jesus, Light of Confessors,
Jesus, Purity of Virgins,
Jesus, Crown of all Saints,

Have mercy upon us.

Be merciful unto us,
Spare us, O Lord Jesus.
Be merciful unto us,
Hear us, O Lord Jesus.

From all evil,
From all sin,
From Thy wrath,
From the snares of the devil,
From the spirit of fornication,
From everlasting death,
From the neglect of Thy holy Inspirations,
By the mystery of Thy holy Incarnation,
By Thy Nativity,
By Thine Infancy,
By Thy most divine Life,
By Thy labours,
By Thine Agony and Passion,
By Thy Cross and Desolation,
By Thy Sufferings,
By Thy Death and Burial,
By Thy Resurrection,
By Thy Ascension,
By Thy Joys,
By Thy Glory,

Jesus, deliver us.

O LAMB of GOD, that takest away the sins of the
world :
JESUS, spare us.
O LAMB of GOD, that takest away the sins of the
world :
JESUS, graciously hear us.
O LAMB of GOD, that takest away the sins of the
world :
JESUS, have mercy on us.

JESUS, hear us :
JESUS, graciously hear us.

Let us pray.

O LORD JESUS CHRIST, Who hast said, Ask
and ye shall receive ; seek and ye shall find ;
knock and it shall be opened unto you ; grant we
beseech Thee, to our most humble supplications,
the gift of Thy most divine Love, that we may ever
love Thee with our whole hearts, words, and works,
and never cease to praise Thee.

LITANY OF REPENTANCE.

LORD, have mercy upon us.
    CHRIST, have mercy upon us.
LORD, have mercy upon us.
O CHRIST, hear us.
O CHRIST, graciously hear us.
O GOD the FATHER, of Heaven,
O GOD the Son, Redeemer of the world,
O GOD the HOLY GHOST,
O HOLY TRINITY, One GOD,

Have mercy upon us.

O GOD, Who wouldest not the death of a sinner, but rather that he should be converted and live,

Who didst not spare the Angels that sinned, but didst cast them down to hell,

Who didst call Adam after his fall to acknowledgment of his sin and to repentance,

Who didst save Noah and Lot from the destruction of the ungodly,

Who didst fearfully punish Pharaoh, feigning repentance, yet hardened in heart,

Who forgavest the sins of Thy disobedient people at the prayer of Moses,

Who didst spare the Ninevites when they repented with fasting,

Who by the prophet Nathan, didst bring David to acknowledge his sin,

Who didst put away his sin when he humbly confessed it,

Who didst spare even Ahab when he humbled himself and repented,

Who heardest Judith as she prayed in sackcloth and ashes,

Who deliveredst Hezekiah and his people when he fasted and prayed,

Who didst hear and pardon penitent Manasseh,

Who camest into the world to save sinners,

Who sentest as Thy herald, John, the preacher of repentance,

Who didst absolve the woman taken in adultery,

Who forgavest the many sins of Mary Magdalen, who loved much,

Who didst restore the penitent Peter,

Who didst receive publicans and sinners, and didst eat with them,

Who didst call Saul the persecutor to repentance,
Who didst send Thine Apostles to preach
repentance,
O God, the Gracious and Merciful, slow
to anger, and of great kindness, Who re-
pentest Thee of the evil,

Have mercy upon us.

Be favourable :
Spare us, good Lord.
Be favourable :
Graciously hear us, good Lord.

From all sin and evil,
From a sudden and impenitent death,
By Thy Baptism and Fasting,
By Thy toils and griefs,
By Thy Precious Blood,
In the hour of death and in the Day of
Judgment,

Good Lord, deli-ver us.

We sinners do beseech Thee to hear us, and
that it may please Thee to bring us to true
repentance,
That we may judge ourselves, and bring forth
worthy fruits of penance,
That we may chasten our bodies and bring
them into subjection, so that sin may not
reign in our mortal bodies,
That, being dead unto sin, we may live unto
righteousness,
That we may work out our own salvation
with fear and trembling,
That, coming boldly to the throne of grace, we
may obtain mercy and find grace to help in
time of need,
That we may count all things but loss for
Christ,
That it may please Thee to correct and to
purge us in time, and to spare us in

We beseech Thee to hear us, good Lord.

Son of God,
We beseech Thee to hear us.
O Lamb of God, that takest away the sins of the
world :
Spare us, good Lord.
O Lamb of God, That takest away the sins of the
world :
Graciously hear us, O Lord.
O Lamb of God, That takest away the sins of the
world :
Have mercy upon us.
O Christ, hear us :
O CHRIST, graciously hear us.
Lord, have mercy upon us :
CHRIST, have mercy upon us.
Lord, have mercy upon us.
Have mercy upon me, O God, after Thy great
goodness.
Have mercy upon me, O Lord, have mercy upon
me.

Let us pray.

O GOD, Who castest out none, but of Thy
gracious Goodness art favourable to sinners,
however great, when they repent ; mercifully regard
the prayers of Thy humble servants, that they may
have strength to fulfil Thy commandments.

O God, Who desireth not the death, but the
repentance of sinners, most pitifully regard the weakness of our mortal nature, and in Thy loving-kindness
prosper all our endeavours, that of Thine infinite
mercy we may obtain remission of all our sins, steadfastness in Thy service, and finally, with joy, the reward
which Thou hast promised unto them that persevere
unto the end ; through Jesus Christ our Lord.
Amen.

LITANY OF THE BLESSED SACRAMENT.

GOD the FATHER, of Heaven,
God the SON, Redeemer of the world,
God the HOLY GHOST,
Holy Trinity, One GOD,
Living Bread, Hidden GOD and SAVIOUR,
Ever-abiding Sacrifice, Pure Oblation,
Lamb without spot,
Food of Angels, Hidden Manna, Word made
 Flesh,
Cup of Blessing, Mystery of Faith,
Heavenly Medicine, Gift exceeding all fulness,
Pledge of future Glory,
Have mercy upon us.

Be merciful, hear us, O LORD JESUS,
Be merciful, spare us, O LORD JESUS,

From an unworthy reception of Thy Body and
 Blood,
From the vanity of the world, the lusts of the flesh,
 the works of the devil,
From all occasion of sin,
By the desire with which Thou didst desire to
 eat the Passover with Thy disciples,
By the humility with which Thou didst wash
 Thy disciples' feet,
By the ardent charity with which Thou didst
 institute this Divine Sacrament,
By Thy precious Blood, Which we receive in this
 Mystery.
By Thy Body, Which was wounded for our
 transgressions,
Good Lord, deliver us.

We beseech Thee to hear us ; and that it may
   please Thee to increase our love, devotion, and
   reverence to Thee in these Holy Mysteries,
That Thou wouldst lead us through faith and
   penitence to a frequent use of this Blessed
   Sacrament,
That Thou wouldst impart to us all the precious
   and heavenly fruits of this life-giving Sacrifice,
That Thou wouldst preserve us from all heresy,
   unbelief, or hardness of heart,
That Thou wouldst strengthen us at the hour of
   our death with this heavenly Nourishment,

We beseech Thee to hear us.

O LAMB of GOD, That takest away the sins of the
   world,
Have mercy upon us.
O LAMB of GOD, That takest away the sins of the
   world,
Have mercy upon us.
O LAMB of GOD, That takest away the sins of the
   world,
Grant us Thy peace.

   O CHRIST, hear us.
   O CHRIST, graciously hear us.

Our FATHER.

   Thou hast given us Bread from heaven,
   Filled with all sweetness and delight.

O GOD, Who in Thy wonderful Sacrament hast
   left us a perpetual Memorial of Thy Passion,
grant us, we beseech Thee, so to reverence the sacred
Mysteries of Thy Body and Blood, that we may continually perceive in our souls the fruit of Thy Redemption, Who with the FATHER and the HOLY
GHOST, livest and reignest, world without end.
Amen.

   LORD, hear our prayer,
   And let our cry come unto Thee.

✠ GOD the FATHER, GOD the SON, GOD the HOLY GHOST, bless, preserve, and keep us now and at the hour of death. Amen.

LITANY OF THE PASSION.

LORD, have mercy upon us :
     CHRIST, have mercy upon us :
LORD, have mercy upon us.
O CHRIST, hear us :
O CHRIST, graciously hear us.
O GOD the FATHER, of Heaven,
O GOD the SON, Redeemer of the world,
O GOD the HOLY GHOST,
O HOLY TRINITY, One GOD,
JESUS, Who didst institute the Holy Sacrament of the Altar in memory of Thy Passion,
JESUS, going forth from the upper chamber to give Thyself to death,
JESUS, praying in the Garden of Olives,
JESUS, overcome with heaviness, strengthened by an Angel in Thine Agony and Sweat of Blood,
JESUS, sold and betrayed by Judas,
JESUS, taken and bound by soldiers,
JESUS, forsaken by Thy disciples,
JESUS, dragged through the streets of Jerusalem, and led from one tribunal to another as a malefactor,
JESUS, accused by false witnesses,
JESUS, outraged, struck, and insulted, during the whole night,
JESUS, denied by Saint Peter,
JESUS, led before Pilate, and accused by the Jews,
JESUS, despised by Herod,
JESUS, to Whom Barabbas was preferred by the people, and Whose Death they demanded,
JESUS, scourged,

Have mercy upon us.

JESUS, clothed with purple, crowned with thorns,
with a reed in Thy Hand, and treated as a
mock King,

JESUS, spit upon,

JESUS, brought before the people,

JESUS, condemned to death by Pilate,

JESUS, laden with the Cross, and led to Calvary,

JESUS, stripped of Thy garments,

JESUS, nailed to the Cross,

JESUS, blasphemed on the Cross,

JESUS, Who didst pray for Thine enemies,

JESUS, Who didst promise Paradise to the penitent thief,

JESUS, Who didst commend to each other Thy
Mother and Saint John,

JESUS, Who didst say to Thy Father, MY GOD,
MY GOD, why hast Thou forsaken Me?

JESUS, Who didst taste vinegar in Thy thirst,

JESUS, Who didst say, It is finished,

JESUS, Who didst commend Thy Spirit to Thy
FATHER,

JESUS, bowing Thine Head upon the Cross,

JESUS, giving up the Ghost,

JESUS, dead upon the Cross,

JESUS, pierced with a spear,

JESUS, shedding Blood and Water from Thy Side,

JESUS, taken down from the Cross, and laid in
Thy Mother's arms,

JESUS, laid in the tomb,

JESUS, obedient unto death,

JESUS, destroying death by Thy Death,

JESUS, King of Glory,

Have mercy upon us.

O LAMB of GOD, That takest away the sins of the world:
Spare us, good Lord.

O LAMB of GOD, That takest away the sins of the
world :
Graciously hear us, good Lord.

O LAMB of GOD, That takest away the sins of the
world :
Have mercy upon us.
O CHRIST, hear us :
O CHRIST, graciously hear us.
LORD, have mercy upon us :
CHRIST, have mercy upon us :
LORD, have mercy upon us.
We adore Thee, O CHRIST, and we bless Thee,
*Because by Thy Cross and Passion Thou hast redeemed
the world.*

Let us pray.

O LORD, Who, for the redemption of the world,
wast pleased to be born, to be circumcised,
to be rejected by the Jews, to be betrayed by
the traitor Judas with a kiss, to be bound with
thongs, to be led as an innocent Lamb to the
slaughter, and to be shamefully presented to the gaze
of Annas, Caiaphas, Pilate, and Herod ; to be accused by false witnesses, to be insulted with scourgings and revilings, to be spit upon and crowned with
thorns, to be buffeted upon the Face and struck with a
reed, to be blindfolded, to be stripped of Thy clothes,
to be fastened with nails to the cross, to be lifted up
thereon, to be reckoned among thieves, to have gall
and vinegar given Thee to drink, and to be pierced
with a lance ; through these Thy most holy Sufferings,
which we, Thy unworthy servants, devoutly call to
mind, and by Thy holy Cross and by Thy Death,
deliver us from the pains of hell, and vouchsafe to
conduct us whither Thou didst conduct the thief who
was crucified with Thee, Who, with the FATHER
and the HOLY GHOST, livest and reignest, ever One
GOD, world without end.   Amen.

Offices.

Offices

*Which may be said in common by Communicants
before and after the Celebration.*

PREPARATION BEFORE HOLY COMMUNION.

(All standing up, let the Reader say the Antiphon.)

REMEMBER not, LORD, our offences, nor the
offences of our forefathers, neither take Thou
vengeance of our sins.

PSALM LXXXIV. *Quam dilecta!*

O HOW amiable are Thy dwellings : Thou LORD
of hosts !

My soul hath a desire and longing to enter into
the courts of the LORD : my heart and my flesh rejoice
in the living GOD.

Yea, the sparrow hath found her an house, and
the swallow a nest where she may lay her young :
even Thy altars, O LORD of hosts, my King and
my GOD.

Blessed are they that dwell in Thy house : they
will be alway praising Thee :

Blessed is the man whose strength is in Thee : in
whose heart are Thy ways.

Who going through the vale of misery use it for a
well : and the pools are filled with water.

They will go from strength to strength : and

unto the GOD of gods appeareth every one of them in Sion.

O LORD GOD of hosts, hear my prayer : hearken, O GOD of Jacob.

Behold, O GOD our Defender : and look upon the face of Thine Anointed.

For one day in Thy courts : is better than a thousand.

I had rather be a door-keeper in the house of my GOD : than to dwell in the tents of ungodliness.

For the LORD GOD is a Light and Defence : the LORD will give grace and worship, and no good thing shall he withhold from them that live a godly life.

O LORD GOD of hosts : blessed is the man that putteth his trust in Thee.

Glory be to the FATHER, &c.

PSALM CXXX. *De profundis.*

OUT of the deep have I called upon Thee, O LORD : LORD, hear my voice.

O let Thine ears consider well : the voice of my complaint.

If Thou, LORD, wilt be extreme to mark what is done amiss : O LORD, who may abide it ?

For there is mercy with Thee : therefore shalt Thou be feared.

I look for the LORD ; my soul doth wait for Him : in His word is my trust.

My soul fleeth unto the LORD : before the morning watch, I say, before the morning watch.

O Israel, trust in the LORD, for with the LORD there is mercy ; and with Him is plenteous redemption.

And He shall redeem Israel : from all his sins.

Glory be to the FATHER, &c.

(All repeat the Antiphon).

REMEMBER not, LORD, our offences, nor the offences of our forefathers, neither take Thou vengeance of our sins.

> LORD, have mercy upon us.
> *CHRIST, have mercy upon us.*
> LORD, have mercy upon us.

Our FATHER.

I SAID, LORD, have mercy upon me :
> *Heal my soul, for I have sinned against Thee.*
Turn Thee again, O LORD, at the last :
> *And be gracious unto Thy servants.*
Let Thy mercy, O LORD, be shewed upon us :
> *As we do put our trust in Thee.*
Let Thy priests be clothed with righteousness :
> *And let Thy saints sing with joyfulness.*
Cleanse Thou me from my secret faults :
> *And keep Thy servant from presumptuous sins.*
O LORD, hear my prayer :
> *And let my cry come unto Thee.*
The LORD be with you :
> *And with thy spirit.*

Let us pray.

O MOST merciful GOD, incline Thy merciful ears to our prayers, and enlighten our hearts with the grace of the HOLY SPIRIT, that we may worthily minister at, and worthily approach, Thy Holy Mysteries, and love Thee with an everlasting love, through JESUS CHRIST. Amen.

O LORD, we beseech Thee, visit and cleanse our consciences, that Thy SON our LORD JESUS CHRIST may, when He cometh, find in us a dwelling-place prepared for Him, Who liveth and reigneth with Thee in the Unity of the HOLY GHOST, ever one GOD, world without end. Amen.

ALMIGHTY GOD, unto Whom all hearts be open, all desires known, and from Whom no secrets are hid ; cleanse the thoughts of our hearts by the inspiration of Thy HOLY SPIRIT, that we may perfectly love Thee, and worthily magnify Thy Holy Name, through CHRIST our Lord.   Amen.

BURN up with the fire of Thy HOLY SPIRIT, O LORD, our hearts and reins, that we may serve Thee with a pure body, and please Thee with a clean heart, through JESUS CHRIST our LORD. Amen.

LET the Comforter which proceedeth from Thee, O LORD, enlighten our minds, we beseech Thee, and lead us, as Thy SON hath promised, into all truth ; through the same Thy SON, JESUS CHRIST. Amen.

WE beseech Thee, O LORD, let the virtue of Thy HOLY SPIRIT be present with us through Thy mercy, to cleanse our hearts, and protect us against all adversities ; through JESUS CHRIST. Amen.

GOD, Who didst teach the hearts of Thy faithful people, by the sending to them the light of Thy Holy Spirit ; Grant us by the same Spirit to have a right judgment in all things, and evermore to rejoice in His holy comfort ; through the merits of CHRIST JESUS our SAVIOUR, Who liveth and reigneth with Thee, in the unity of the same Spirit, one GOD, world without end.   Amen.

ALMIGHTY Everlasting GOD, lo ! we approach to the Sacrament of Thy Only-Begotten SON, our LORD JESUS CHRIST ; we approach sick to the Physician of life, unclean to the Fountain of mercy,

blind to the Light of eternal brightness, poor and
needy to the LORD of heaven and earth : we pray
Thee, therefore, of the abundance of Thy boundless
bounty, that Thou wouldest vouchsafe to heal our
sickness, to wash our defilements, to enlighten our
blindness, to enrich our poverty, to clothe our nakedness ; that we may receive the Bread of Angels, the
King of kings and Lord of lords, with such reverence
and humility, such contrition and devotion, such
purity and faith, such purpose and intention, as is
expedient for the health of our souls. Grant us, we
beseech Thee, that we may receive not only the
Sacrament of the Body and Blood of the Lord, but
the Substance also and virtue of the Sacrament. O
most gracious GOD, grant us so to receive the Body of
Thy Only-Begotten SON, our LORD JESUS CHRIST,
which He took of the Virgin Mary, that we may be
found worthy to be incorporated into His mystical
Body, and accounted among His members. O most
loving FATHER, grant unto us, that Whom now we
purpose to receive veiled in our pilgrimage, we may,
at length, with unveiled face, contemplate for ever,
even Thy well-beloved SON, Who with Thee, liveth
and reigneth in the Unity of the Holy Ghost, One
GOD, throughout all ages. Amen.

JOY with peace, amendment of life, space for true
repentance, the grace and consolation of Thy
Holy Spirit, perseverance in good works, a contrite
and humbled heart, and a happy consummation of
our lives, grant to us, O Almighty and merciful LORD.
Amen.

THANKSGIVING AFTER HOLY COMMUNION.

(*Antiphon.*)

Let us sing the hymn of the three children, which those blessed ones sang in the furnace of fire, praising GOD.

Benedicite: omnia opera.

O ALL ye works of the LORD, bless ye the LORD : praise Him, and magnify Him for ever.

O ye angels of the LORD, bless ye the LORD : praise Him and magnify Him for ever.

O let Israel bless the LORD : praise Him, and magnify Him for ever.

O ye priests of the LORD, bless ye the LORD : praise Him, and magnify Him for ever.

O ye servants of the LORD, bless ye the LORD : praise Him, and magnify Him for ever.

O ye spirits and souls of the righteous, bless ye the LORD : praise Him, and magnify Him for ever.

O ye holy and humble men of heart, bless ye the LORD : praise Him, and magnify Him for ever.

O Ananias, Azarias, and Misael, bless ye the LORD : praise Him, and magnify Him for ever.

PSALM CL. *Laudate Dominum.*

O PRAISE GOD in His holiness : praise Him in the firmament of His power.

Praise Him in His noble acts : praise Him according to His excellent greatness.

Praise Him in the sound of the trumpet : praise Him upon the lute and harp.

Praise Him in the cymbals and dances : praise Him upon the strings and pipe.

Praise Him upon the well-tuned cymbals : praise Him upon the loud cymbals.

Let every thing that hath breath: praise the
LORD.

Glory be to the FATHER, &c.

(All repeat the Antiphon.)

Let us sing the hymn of the three children, which
those blessed ones sang in the furnace of fire,
praising GOD.

Let us pray.

LORD, have mercy upon us.
CHRIST, have mercy upon us.
LORD, have mercy upon us.
Our FATHER.

Let all Thy works praise Thee, O LORD :
And Thy saints give thanks unto Thee.
Thy saints shall exult in glory :
They shall rejoice in their beds.
Not unto us, O LORD : not unto us :
But to Thy Name give glory.
LORD, hear our prayer :
And let our cry come unto Thee.
The LORD be with you :
And with Thy spirit.

Let us pray.

O GOD, Who didst to the three children soothe
the flames of fire, mercifully grant that the
flames of sin may not kindle upon us, Thy servants.
Amen.

PREVENT us, O LORD, in all our doings, with
Thy most gracious favour, and further us with
Thy continual help, that in all our works, begun, con-

tinued, and ended in Thee, we may glorify Thy Holy Name, and finally, by Thy mercy, obtain everlasting life ; through JESUS CHRIST our LORD. Amen.

O GOD, Who in this wonderful Sacrament hast left us a perpetual Memorial of Thy Passion ; grant us, we beseech Thee, so to reverence these sacred Mysteries of Thy Body and Blood, that we may continually perceive in our souls the fruit of Thy Redemption ; Who, with the FATHER and the HOLY GHOST, livest and reignest, world without end. Amen.

WE render Thee thanks, O LORD, Holy FATHER, Almighty, Everlasting GOD, Who hast vouchsafed not for any desert of ours, but only out of the condescension of Thy mercy, to feed us sinners, Thy unworthy servants, with the precious Body and Blood of Thy SON our LORD JESUS CHRIST ; and we pray that this holy Communion may not bring guilt upon us to condemnation, but may intercede for us to our pardon and salvation ; let it be to us an armour of faith, and a shield of good purpose ; a riddance of all vices ; an extermination of evil desires and longings ; an increase of love and patience, of humility and obedience, and all virtues ; a firm defence against the wiles of our enemies, visible and invisible ; a perfect quieting of all our impulses, fleshly and spiritual ; a firm adherence to Thee, the one true GOD, and a blessed consummation of our end ; and we pray Thee, that Thou wouldest vouchsafe to bring us sinners to that ineffable Feast, where Thou, with Thy SON and the HOLY SPIRIT, art to Thy servants a true Light, full Satiety, everlasting Joy, Pleasure consummated, and perfect Happiness ; through the same our LORD JESUS CHRIST. Amen.

WE beseech Thee, O LORD JESUS CHRIST, that Thy Passion may be unto us virtue, whereby we may be fenced, protected, and defended. Let the sprinkling of Thy Blood be to us the washing away of all our sins. Let Thy Death be to us everlasting glory, both now and for ever. Amen.

THE Grace of our LORD JESUS CHRIST, and the Love of GOD, and the Fellowship of the Holy Ghost, be with us all evermore. Amen.

LONDON : PRINTED BY
SPOTTISWOODE AND CO., NEW-STREET SQUARE
AND PARLIAMENT STREET